It is an original concept with subject matter children can relate to. Children will be fascinated by the underwater world of beautiful creatures and the dangers of diving. They'll relate to the friendships and compassion, using the characters as role models. An exceptional story.
(*Barbara Sorby, former Manager of Sheffield School Library Service*)

This book is a thrilling adventure about Lucy and her friends, Jack and Solomon. It's an exciting book and it is also a great idea to add in the pictures and information about the sea creatures that are mentioned in the book in the back of it. If you like books with cliff hangers everywhere - look no further. I really enjoyed this book and I can't wait to read the next one in the series.
(Dylan, aged 10)

Lucy is a brave girl who took a big step and tried something new. Lucy loves adventures. I like the way she made new friends and sometimes put herself in danger to help her friends.
(Susannah, age 11)

Lucy is a girl who never gives up her fight for what she believes in. She shows that we can make adults aware of problems and children can make a difference to the planet.
Esme (aged 9)

The author's passion and knowledge of the natural world really shines through in her writing.
(Eleanor H. – children's author)

Great characters … compelling story … altogether a brilliant read.
(Julie, Primary teacher)

This is a brilliant book. I meant to flick through it before giving it to my grandson of 10 years. However, it was so well written, I could not put it down. Very inspiring, thought provoking and imagination- triggering! I know my grandson will be enthralled.
(Dorothy, Grandma)

This is a perfect book for the age group ... a really good story that teachers will love to read to their classes, and children will hassle their parents to buy for them. I love it.
(Andrew L, Primary School Education Consultant)

The author manages to combine an exciting adventure with the environmental concerns a young girl has about ocean creatures. A very current theme and beautifully written. *(Chloe -Year 4 teacher)*

For
Charlotte (age 11)
who was the first
to read and love this story.

First published in 2020 by
Footprint to the Future Books

ISBN   978-1-8380643-0-3
First published January 2020
Edition 2 (illustrated) published May 2020

Footprint to the Future
is a social enterprise producing teaching resources and
books for children and adults to help everyone understand
Planet Earth.

Footprint to the Future Books
Holland House, 165 London Road, Temple Ewell, Kent,
CT16 3DA

www.footprinttothefuture.co.uk

Eye of the Turtle

GLORIA BARNETT

A Lucy Morgan Adventure Story

Illustrated by Katrin Lamb

Footprint to the Future Books

PART 1

CHAPTER ONE

London

Bang! The front door slammed shut and keys clattered on the hall table.

As Mum burst into the room, my peace vanished. The cosy cushions in my reading den collapsed into a heap around me. My book slipped from my hand and hit the floor with a dull thud. I tried to stand up but fell back on the floor as my blanket turned into a green snake curling and twisting around my ankles.

'You'll never guess what's happened.' Her voice was trembling.

'They're closing my library,' she said, 'I can't believe it. It's one of the best community libraries in London, we help so many people ... and they're closing us down.' Her eyes were glistening as she blinked and screwed up her face, trying to stop tears from escaping, but she lost the battle and droplets ran together like tiny rivers down her cheeks.

Maggie shuffled out of the kitchen. Her comfortable slippers were too big for her scrawny, old feet. She took a long look at Mum and frowned.

'Tea,' she said, 'that's what you need.' She turned back towards the kitchen.

'I'm losing my job!' said Mum, her voice was so quiet I could hardly hear her. She seemed heart-broken. Tears reached her chin.

I needed to give Mum a hug, but my blanket snake wouldn't let go. My fingers pulled and pulled and gradually I loosened the blanket and fought my way free. I gave her a big cuddle. It was a bit clumsy but was the best I could do. Mum didn't cry very often so I wasn't quite sure what to do next. Was I supposed to say something? The silence seemed to last forever. When she spoke first, I breathed a sigh of relief.

'I'm sorry Lucy, but I don't know what we're going to do.'

'It's alright, Mum,' I said, 'I'm sure we'll think of something.' I tried to sound positive, but my brain was completely empty of ideas.

Maggie brought in the tea. She'd only walked a few feet from the kitchen, yet she noisily puffed air out of her mouth as she sat down in the armchair. She listened quietly, as Mum explained what had happened.

'Don't you go worrying now,' said Maggie, calmly. 'I'm sure it'll be fine.'

She struggled to get to her feet again. 'These things always sort themselves out. I'll pop back next door and tell Stan what's going on. He might have some ideas on what you could do next.'

I didn't hold out much hope that Stan would come up with an answer to Mum's problems. He spent most of the day in front of the television, watching quiz and gardening programmes, though goodness knows what use he had for gardening information. He didn't have a garden. He might have been a bit old, but I did love him and Maggie, and I'd spent every day with them after school for years now, waiting until Mum got home from work.

Mum's mood slowly improved as she calmed down, but I wasn't sure what was going through her mind. She looked through the window, muttering, then turned towards me.

'Perhaps this is an opportunity. Perhaps we can begin to think differently, go in a new direction?'

The window rattled and she turned to watch the wind battering rain against the glass.

'There's nothing special for us here, Lucy. It's cold and damp. Look down. There's hardly a tree in sight. This isn't leafy green London, full of royal parks and palaces. We're living on the twelfth floor of a concrete block. We're breathing in fumes from the motorway. This isn't the life I want for us.'

Mum looked away from the window, sat up straight and pulled her shoulders back. 'We need to make a BIG decision.'

She sprang to her feet. Her tall, thin body paced up and down like a captive tiger in a cage. Was she nervous or excited?

'We should get away from here. I'll find a better job. We'll improve our lives!' She pushed her long blonde hair away from her face and smiled.

Somehow, I didn't expect to see Mum smile so soon after her shattering news. Words came tumbling uncontrollably out of her mouth. I only caught a few phrases. Great opportunity! Live somewhere warm! Move away!

Move away? Where to? I've lived in London for every second of my eleven years. I know nothing about anywhere else! My fingers twisted in my long hair. I watched her closely as she calmed down, but I couldn't tell what was on her mind.

'I can email the job agency to search for a new job, but I've got an idea, so first I want to look at some big maps.'

She wiped tears away as she made her plans. 'We'll pop downtown to the main library.' She looked at her watch. 'Good, they don't close for another hour yet.'

Wrapped up warmly against the chilly east wind we hurried down the hill to the High Street. The old library building loomed above us and I rushed inside to the warmth.

Mum settled in with the reference books, so I wandered into the children's library. I looked at their display of new children's stories, then curled up in a bean bag, reading a book by one of my favourite authors. I hoped Mum would find what she needed, then perhaps our lives could return to normal.

The clock was ticking towards closing time when she came looking for me.

'I've found what I wanted,' she said, her face crinkled with excitement.

'Great,' I replied, but I'd no idea what she'd been looking for. 'Can we go home now?'

'Might as well. I can email from home, though it might be days before I get any replies.'

'It's here!' she squealed, staring at her iPad.

'What's here?' I asked, although I had a fair idea. It was nearly a week since our library trip, and she'd been checking her emails about once a minute ever since.

'It's the answer I've been hoping for!' she explained. 'It's a job! I've been offered a new job!'

I'd never seen her smile so widely. 'Great.' I mirrored her smile. This was obviously good news. Mum needed a job.

'It's amazing!' she said, 'I've been offered a job in a new Community Library and I'll be helping the staff to run the English Language classes.'

'You'll love that,' I said. 'Helping people is what you're good at and there's lots of people in London who don't speak very good English.'

'Well, yes.' She hesitated and looked away from me, 'but it's not quite as simple as a job just around the corner, Lucy. It's ... it's not in London.'

'Where is it then?'

'Well, the job is on Pontus Island,' she said quietly.

'Where on earth is that? I've never heard of it.'

'It's in the Caribbean,' she explained.

'The Caribbean!' I could hear my voice echoing loudly around the quiet room. 'That's the other side of the world isn't it?' My thoughts were spinning around, trying to make sense of what was happening. 'But ... we'll be leaving everything we know ... to move to a strange country!'

'I know,' she said, smiling, 'isn't it exciting? We can start again. A new beginning.'

My brain was in overload. My palms went clammy and I began to shake with panic. I'd be leaving my school, my friends ... and our neighbours, Maggie and Stan ... they were like the grandparents I didn't have. I'd be leaving London to travel thousands of miles away ... and I'd never see them ... or my friends ever again.

CHAPTER TWO

Sharing the News

Mum was bouncing around the flat, her feet hardly touching the ground. 'It'll be such a different world compared to here,' she said, excitedly.

My brain had gone fuzzy and I couldn't think straight. 'Mum!' I yelled and just for a moment she stood still.

'What's up, Lucy?' She looked startled.

'Everything! We'll be moving away from everything I know, to go somewhere I can't even imagine. My life is never going to be normal again.'

She came closer and put her arm around my shoulders and hugged me tight.

'Oh, don't worry love,' she said calmly, 'we'll be fine. You'll soon make new friends at a different school. It'll be such an adventure. We can change our lives. I've already checked the price of the air fare to Pontus and my redundancy money will buy us one-way tickets to fly out there.'

My heart skipped a beat. I heard myself yelling again. 'WHAT?' You're going to spend the only money we've got … on one-way tickets? That means we can't even change our minds and come back if we don't like it!'

'It's okay ... we're going to love it there,' said Mum, smiling.

I was stunned. Was there anything I could do or say to stop all this happening?

Mum suggested we go next door to tell Maggie and Stan our plans.

Maggie opened the door cautiously and seemed surprised to see us.

'Oh, I wasn't expecting anyone to call.' She immediately started smiling and called into the flat. 'Hey, Stan, it's Sarah and Lucy.'

I found Stan sitting in the lounge and gave him a big hug. He switched off the game show he'd been watching on television.

'What's up ladies? You got a problem?'

'No Stan, we're fine, but we've got some exciting news for you,' said Mum, smiling.

Maggie raised an eyebrow, showing the lines on her face. 'C'mon then, tell us all about it,' she said.

'Well, we've decided to move away,' said Mum.

I frowned as I looked across at her. My brain was muttering silently ... I wouldn't call it exciting news .... and YOU'VE decided to move ... not me.

They listened in shocked silence as Mum explained.

'So, you see, it's all for the best. We'll have a better life out there.'

Maggie took time to recover her voice. 'Gosh, I … I can't believe it,' she said. 'We've known you for so long. When you and young Ryan got married and came to live next door, we couldn't have wished for better neighbours. And you, Lucy,' Maggie put her arm around me and squeezed hard, 'we've been looking after you since you were three years old.' She looked straight at me, tears rolling down her cheeks. 'You've practically half-lived with us since your Daddy's accident and your Mummy had to work so hard to look after the two of you.'

Stan looked totally shocked and I realized it wasn't just *our* lives that were going to change.

13

Maggie recovered first. 'Well, you mustn't worry about us,' she said, as supportive as ever. 'We'll be ok. We'll miss you, of course we will, but yes, you need to take this opportunity and try to do something better with your lives. Perhaps we could come out for a holiday and see you when you've settled in.'

Stan was nodding, but I felt I was deserting them. Pontus was thousands of miles away, and I wasn't sure if Maggie and Stan could manage the journey.

'They looked so sad about us leaving,' I said, as we walked back to our flat.

'I know,' said Mum, 'they've been so good to us over the years, and I'm really going to miss them, but we need to go, Lucy. This is our life and now is the right time for us to do this. We need to move on and have a new goal for our lives.'

My teeth were biting against each other and my jaw felt tight. Mum seemed so sure about everything, but I was finding moments when her big idea was difficult to cope with.

A few days later I shared my secret with Eve and Nayla at school.

We were alone during lunchtime, so I took a deep breath, lifted my chin and spoke out. 'My Mum's decided we're moving away from London,' I said.

'What? ... you can't leave us.' Eve wailed.

'We'll probably never see you again,' squealed Nayla. 'Once you've gone, you won't get a chance to come back, you know. Since my parents brought my family here from Pakistan, we've never been able to afford to travel back home. I really miss all my aunties and cousins.'

'Well, that doesn't apply to me,' I said. 'I don't have any relatives to miss anyway.' I shrugged my shoulders, trying not to show I was nervous about going. I pushed thoughts of Maggie and Stan into the far corners of my brain. They weren't related to me, but I knew I would miss them.'

Eve touched my arm, leaned forward and spoke quietly. 'Well, I shall miss you, but at least you'll get away from those nasty girls in the playground who make fun of the block of flats where you live.'

'Nobody ever says anything good about the Bamford Estate. Even my Mum calls it a concrete monstrosity, but our flat is comfy, and I really love the colourful graffiti and all those crazy patterns the older kids have added to the walls.'

We made promises to text each other and stay friends forever, but deep down I knew that once I'd gone, I was probably never going to see them again.

On my last day at school, when my teacher announced I was leaving, some of the other pupils looked quite shocked. I didn't want to cry or show in any way that I felt upset or worried about going. 'Don't worry about me,' I said, 'I'm heading off to live in a wonderful place.'

I couldn't believe what I was saying, but by smiling and with my eyes stretched wide, I managed to look positive and excited. This false attitude acted as my shield and hid my nervousness, but inside my nerves were rattling. I had never been so scared.

CHAPTER THREE

Leaving

Mum bought two second-hand suitcases for our clothes. 'They're a bit battered,' she said, 'but it doesn't matter as we're only going to use them once. We'll be off in a couple of days. Isn't it exciting?'

I couldn't believe my ears. A couple of days! This was all happening much too fast.

Just as I was wondering how I could pack all my favourite things into one small suitcase, Mum started chattering about the importance of throwing all our old things away. What was I going to take with me?

I looked around my small bedroom. Everything was neatly arranged. My books were all lined up on the shelves alongside the games, and the jigsaws were all in their correct boxes. When I dusted my bedroom, I always moved some of my old baby toys around on their shelf. I loved the little wooden people and would put them in their bus or had them walking back towards their house. I would rearrange them so they could play out their pretend lives for another week.

I decided I must have played with some of these toys when Dad was still alive. I really didn't want to get rid of anything I could associate with his memory, but I had to be strong minded. At eleven years old I knew it made sense to send it all to a local nursery school, but I looked again at the little wooden people. I reached up and searched for the small wooden 'daddy' toy. I squeezed it in my hand for a moment, then tucked it inside the suitcase. A thought arrived in my brain with a thud. I would reach Pontus with hardly any possessions at all. I'd have almost nothing to show for my life so far.

The day came and I watched our furniture being taken out to the charity shop van. Our home was looking very strange. The empty rooms echoed as I walked around, and I shivered. It was cold in the flat because the front door had been left open for so long.

I couldn't stop shivering. It was a strange feeling. My home had disappeared. My comfy bed, the bedside light which frightened away the darkness, and even my favourite mug had suddenly been taken away. I felt empty and unsure of myself.

Stan and Maggie had offered to take the keys back to the housing office for us. They were crying, as first they hugged Mum and then hugged me. I could feel the tears forming in my eyes and falling down my cheeks as I buried my face in their warm clothes and clung to each of them.

Mum was being amazingly strong. 'We've got our memories to take with us,' she said quietly, 'that's all we need. Just the two of us and our memories.'

As Mum and I walked down the road to the bus stop, carrying our suitcases, a light drizzly rain started to fall.

Mum didn't look back, but I couldn't resist turning to take one last look. I could see my favourite piece of graffiti on our building, with its bright orange paint pretending to be flames inside a large green triangle. I looked up at the drizzly grey sky and silently said goodbye.

CHAPTER FOUR

The Other Side of the World

'We've definitely reached the Caribbean,' said Mum. 'Look down, you can see the amazing blue of the ocean. It's exactly how I imagined it.'

I hadn't spent any time imagining it over the past few weeks. I'd constantly hoped Mum would change her mind about moving so far away from home. I thought about my friends at school in London and how I was leaving them behind. A sadness clung to all my thoughts. No-one would be friends with me now, a strange girl in a strange country.

'The sunlight is reflecting and sparkling on the surface. See how beautiful it is!' Mum poked my arm, but I kept my head in my book. I didn't want to look at any view through the plane window.

She described what she could see, sounding like a narrator of a television travel documentary. 'There are white beaches around the edge of the island and lush green trees and plants everywhere. I've never seen anything so colourful.'

Without moving my head, I took a quick sideways glance out of the window. Clouds were speeding past us. The plane was coming down fast, and we were getting seriously close to the ground ... my brain screened images of planes crashing out of the sky.

As the plane skimmed the tops of the greenery, I saw part of a harbour with fishing boats and yachts and a kaleidoscope of images rushed past. If this had been a holiday trip for just a couple of weeks, I might have been interested in these new sights; I might have felt it was an adventure; I may even have got excited, but this wasn't a holiday; this was scary; this was the unknown.

'We're so close I can see houses and cars,' said Mum, with child-like excitement, 'and a big market bustling with people.' She was speaking as if she'd never seen people before!

I pushed my fingers into my ears, trying to stop the sharp pain that was making me screw my eyes up tight. The plane's undercarriage bounced on the runway, and the brakes pushed us forward in our seats. We'd landed. This was it. I closed my eyes and tried to breathe deeply. We'd arrived.

The air smelt different as we moved towards the open door. My nose twitched. The air which entered my lungs was hot and dry. I struggled to catch my breath as I went down the steps from the plane.

'It's so warm. It's wonderful!' Mum gasped. 'Nothing like drab, cold London.'

I couldn't argue with that, it was very different ... but I'd have given anything to have been back at home, with my school friends and my normal life.

Before we left the UK, Mum had arranged for us to be met at the airport by Robert, the estate agent who'd organised our house search. A tall man stood patiently amongst the crowd as we exited Customs. He held a card with Mum's name written in big letters and smiled as we walked towards him.

Robert was a local ... thin and gangly, with dark skin, curly hair and crooked teeth. He wore a lightweight, white cotton suit and bright blue, flower-patterned, open-necked shirt. He seemed friendly enough and constantly chattered as we walked to his car. As he drove along bumpy roads away from the airport, he explained our surroundings,

19

pointing out fields of sugar cane and plantations of large-leaved banana plants.

'See all those cotton bags hanging around the bananas ... farmers use them to protect the fruit from insects. You won't have seen bananas growing where you've come from.'

My eyes turned skywards. Really? I thought London was famous for its banana growing! I glared at the back of Robert's head.

There were no pavements on the roads or alongside the homes in the villages ... no brick-built housing estates or streets of identical homes like we'd had in London. These buildings were of various shapes, sizes and colours and so many of them were rickety and poorly looked-after. Some didn't even have glass in the windows.

Surely, some of these houses would fall over if I touched them. I began to hope we wouldn't end up with a tumble-down shack like these, with rubble in overgrown gardens.

'Why do some of these houses look like they're collapsing?' Mum asked.

'Oh, those are houses that are waiting to be rebuilt,' said Robert. 'Yeah, they got damaged in the last hurricane.'

Mum looked puzzled.

'What d'you mean … DAMAGED IN THE HURRICANE?' I yelled. 'WHAT HURRICANE?

I'd leant forward with my head between the two front seats. 'Hurricanes are dangerous, aren't they?'

'Yeah, well ... you sort of get used to them,' said Robert. He seemed totally unconcerned. 'We live with the idea of getting some strong winds most years, but it's not always hurricane force, so homes aren't always knocked down. If houses do get damaged, everyone soon comes along and helps rebuild them with new roof tiles and fresh wooden walls. Old stuff gets piled up to one side in case someone can re-use it. I guess most of the homes outside of the city have rubble in their gardens.'

Mum had stopped smiling.

Before she could say anything, Robert spoke up. 'Look, you'll get used to it. We all do. If you live in the Caribbean, it's what happens. Most of the time the hurricanes miss us. It's only every few years that there's a problem ... and usually not many people get hurt.'

I'd heard of hurricanes on the news where falling trees and bits of flying roof hadn't just hurt people ... they'd actually killed them. I couldn't believe what I was hearing. Mum had brought us to a country where there were going to be hurricanes. Our new home could be destroyed before we even got used to living in it. 'Did you know about this?' I stared at Mum. 'Did you know this was a hurricane country?'

'It's alright, Lucy, we'll be fine. I'm sure we will.' Mum's hesitant voice was unconvincing. 'We're here now, we'll soon settle in ... get used to it all.'

'Why, will it be fine, Mum?' I asked loudly. 'Are you imagining we have a protective wall around us? Do you think nothing can harm us? Well, it can.'

Mum turned to scowl at me, so I glared back.

I was desperate to shout that she wasn't being realistic, but it was no good getting angry ... what was the point ... no-one was listening to my worries at all.

'Are we going to have to build our own house from the leftovers from hurricane damage?' I asked Robert.

'No ... no, of course not!' said Robert. 'Your house is fine. It's in a sheltered spot and I've never heard of any hurricane damage in that part of the island.'

I couldn't believe what I was hearing. Robert was being so relaxed about it, and as for Mum ... she obviously had

21

no idea what the problems were, or else she'd never have brought us here.

My right hand reached for my hair, twisting it, pushing it off my face. I looked out of the car window. This was a dump of a place and it probably wouldn't be long before a hurricane decided to visit our side of the island and blow more houses to pieces.

My shoulders drooped, and I fell back into my seat. London seemed so far away.

CHAPTER FIVE

New Home

Robert drove for over an hour, then slowed as he entered a quiet beach-side area.

'The home you've chosen is here, in Jude's Bay, just six miles from the town of St. Stephens,' said Robert, 'so your new job and Lucy's new school are only a short bus ride away.'

I don't want to travel on a stupid bus or go to a stupid new school! My lips were moving but no sound came out.

We were driven into a small road. Phew! This looked a bit better! I counted six wooden-slatted houses all in different colours. They were fairly well looked-after and didn't seem too rickety. They had tidy gardens and low white fences separating the plots. They actually had proper windows with both glass and shutters.

Robert pointed at a light green property, which was trying to camouflage itself by snuggling into the overgrown trees and bushes surrounding the house.

'It's a two-bedroomed bungalow,' he explained, 'all one level inside, but it's built on pillars to raise it off the ground. The steps go up to the balcony, which goes all around the outside and the roof overhangs it to create shade and protects you from rain when you sit outside. We get a little bit of rain every day on Pontus ... it's what keeps the island so green. Yes, I reckon you'll soon be relaxing up there, taking in your new surroundings.'

I noticed a swing settee seat in one corner of the balcony. I climbed the steps and sat down, pushing my feet against the wooden boards, and gently swaying backwards and forwards. The swing was well-built and comfy, with cushioned seats. At least this wasn't wobbly or falling apart.

Robert opened the outside shutters allowing the sun to shine inside. He unlocked the front door and we walked in. It smelt a bit dried up and musty, but a freshening breeze soon rolled in as he opened some windows. It was bigger than our flat in London; one large lounge with a settee and two armchairs; a table and chairs; a kitchen off to one side and a hall leading to two bedrooms and a bathroom.

'This'll be perfect for us, won't it, Lucy?' Mum was smiling at me, being friendly again, so I attempted to smile back. But before I could say anything, Mum was chattering to herself again. 'Soon feel like home,' she said, '... cosy. I'm sure we don't need to worry about hurricanes here, do we?' I decided she was trying to persuade herself by talking out loud.

Well, I wasn't convinced ... this island did NOT feel safe. Perhaps I should stick my head down a nearby rabbit hole ... pretend it wasn't all happening, just ignore the idea of hurricanes! If they don't have rabbits on this island, I'd just have to stick my head under a pillow and close my eyes. I'd deal with all my worries like that. My grumpiness had returned with its noise level at full volume in my brain. I decided I could end up spending the rest of my life under a pillow, in the dark!

Then ... I totally forgot about hurricanes. I was staring at the wall by the kitchen. There was a small green lizard climbing in rapid bursts towards the ceiling.

'What the heck is that?' I yelled. My fingers tingled with cold and the hairs began to twitch along my arms.

'It's okay ... it's just a gecko.' said Robert. He grinned and patted my shoulder. 'It won't hurt you. They're really cool little creatures. They're totally harmless and useful to have in the house too.'

'Really?' I couldn't believe what he was saying, surely lizards were dangerous?

'Yeah, they eat the flies and other insects ... so let the gecko be your friend ... it certainly won't harm you.'

I watched as the little creature clung to the wall, its eyes darting around. I looked around for other wildlife living in my new home.

'Robert, are there any poisonous spiders ... or snakes on this island?' I asked, nervously.

'Ah, that's a good question Lucy.' Mum said and turned to Robert. 'Is there anything dangerous we should worry about, Robert?' she asked.

I sighed, shaking my head. It's a bit late finding out what can eat us or poison us now! You should've asked that question before we left the safety of London. This could be an island full of dinosaurs brought back to life, ones that eat people, like I'd seen in films!

Robert tried to reassure us, 'No, there's nothing here to harm you. Don't worry! I'll leave you to settle in then. Let me know if there's anything else I can help you with.'

Within minutes we were by ourselves.

Unpacking took very little time, as we'd brought scarcely anything with us. Most of our clothes would've been too warm to wear in the heat of Pontus anyway.

Taking Mum's suitcase to her bedroom, it took me only minutes to hang her few clothes in the wardrobe. I put them on the rail with similar colours next to each other, then took my suitcase to my room and put my clothes away tidily. I put my small 'daddy' figure on the bedside table. A crumpled old Zebbie, my favourite toy, fell out of the suitcase onto my bed. I adjusted the zebra's soft, dangly legs so it could sit up. 'There you go, is that comfortable enough for you?'

Zebbie replied with his usual lopsided grin.

'What're you saying?' Mum called from the kitchen. I must have spoken out loud without realizing it. So much had happened in the past twenty-four hours, my brain was spinning around like a tumble drier.

'Can you give me a hand to make the beds please, Lucy?'

Mum had placed a photo frame on her bedside table ... her favourite photo of herself and Dad. His eyes sparkled in the photo and I could understand why Mum described him as having been a happy person. We'd moved a long way from London, but she'd brought her memories with her too.

London seemed like such a long way away. My eyes blinked away the moisture forming beneath my eyelids. I wiped my face with the back of my hand.

'You okay, Lucy?'

I looked away, trying not to show my wet eyes. My stomach felt like it was on a fairground ride, but Mum was still smiling as she looked around.

'I know it all appears very strange,' she said 'but, I think we'll get used to this, won't we?'

Nodding, I tried to smile back at her. Although my stomach had come to the end of its ride, my thoughts continued to tumble.

We had no choice. We'd only bought one-way tickets. We couldn't go back.

Mum glanced at her watch. 'Look, it's five o'clock already. Let's go out and investigate.'

I shrugged and slowly put my shoes back on. I didn't want to go out and explore. Surely, I'd seen enough for one day.

CHAPTER SIX

Dolphin Beach

Crossing the road behind our new home, I saw an enormous wooden sign pointing down a narrow sandy path. 'Dolphin Beach,' it announced, with colourful, cartoon dolphins leaping out of the board on either side of the words.

We turned away from the road. Our steps quickened. As I looked ahead, warm air rushed into my open mouth.

'WOW!'

I'd never been on a beach before, not in my whole life ... ever! It was beautiful! Bleached white sand stretched out ahead, dotted with tall coconut palm trees. The droopy green fronds of the trees created ever-changing shady spots on the sand. The breeze made the leaves dance. The white sand merged with wavelets of gentle, white-topped surf at the edge of the blue waters of the bay.

As my hair blew in the gentle breeze, I swept it behind my ears, keeping my eyes clear to absorb the scene.

'What a view!' My voice was a whisper.

As I walked, my feet sank into the soft warm sand. I took off my shoes and socks. Looking down I saw my toes disappear, but the sand was dry and quickly released my feet as I moved forward.

The beach was quiet and peaceful. A few people sat on sunbeds, under the shade of green umbrellas. Further along, customers were sitting at sunny tables outside a building with signs saying, 'Drifters Restaurant and Bar.'

Mum smiled. 'Let's have a drink there,' she said, 'we can sit and watch the sea. It's called Dolphin Beach, isn't it? We might see dolphins in the sea, jumping and playing? That'd be brilliant ... just what I've imagined.'

We settled at a table with our drinks and gazed across the sand to the water.

It was a stunning view, but there were no signs of any animals leaping from the rippling surface.

The water sparkled in the late afternoon reflections of the sun. I took a deep breath and closed my eyes, letting my senses explore a new world. It was still and quiet. The sun warmed my skin and my nose tried to identify new smells. Perhaps I wouldn't spend my life hiding under a pillow in the dark after all.

A cough disturbed the peace, and I looked behind me.

An old man sat a couple of tables away. He was dark-skinned and dressed in a scruffy shirt with trousers rolled up to just below his knees. His rough feet were tucked into worn leather sandals. The whiskery, silvery-grey growth on his chin wasn't enough to be called a beard. He smiled at me, but I quickly looked away. He was so dishevelled ... I didn't like the look of him.

'Saw you two clinking your glasses together,' said the old man. He had a slow style of talking, with a rich local accent but I was able to understand him if I listened carefully.

His deep voice gave way to an easy laugh and he revealed big gaps between his teeth as he spoke. He leaned forward as if we were sharing a secret.

'You looks like you're celebrating something,' he said.

'Well, actually we are,' said Mum. 'We only arrived on Pontus this morning and moved into a house across the road about an hour ago. We're going to settle here from London.'

The old man got up slowly and brought his drink over to our table. When he removed his big, floppy sunhat he revealed a practically bald, brown head with dark spots on his skin.

'So, you've come to live here? That's really good,' he said, 'we gonna be neighbours then.' His quiet voice got louder the more he smiled.

'Let me introduce myself properly. My name's Joel Browne. Welcome to Jude's Bay. In my opinion, you've come to the best little place on the whole island.'

'Thank you for your warm welcome,' said Mum. 'I'm Sarah Morgan and this is my daughter, Lucy. We're pleased to meet you.'

Why was Mum being so friendly with this scruffy man?

Joel smiled as he spoke. 'If you've only arrived a short while ago, then you gonna have loads'a questions. So, if you don't mind me sitting here, I'll be your friend and guide. C'mon, fire away. Let's see if there is something I can answer.'

He sat down at our table.

I wasn't sure I wanted to get too close to him, let alone ask him anything. Who was this shabby, old man anyway? We were complete strangers to him. Back in London we'd never be so quick to talk to anyone ... in fact, on the underground trains, no-one even smiled at each other. I couldn't even look at his face. I stared at my feet. Why was he trying to be friends with us? His clothes were tatty and torn ... the skin on his feet was dried up, his toenails were cracked and discoloured and how could he walk in such scruffy sandals? I wasn't sure I wanted him as a friend and guide? How could I ever be friends with him?

CHAPTER SEVEN

Ocean Life

Mum took a deep breath.

'Where are the dolphins? How often can we see them? Do they jump out of the sea? How high do they jump? What other animals live in the sea?'

'Whoa,' said Joel, 'stop there. Let me answer some of those questions before you ask any more.'

He wriggled to get comfortable in his seat and looked at Mum closely.

'Them dolphins ... they's very special creatures. They's intelligent, see. They comes into this bay regular and of course, they're mammals. They've not got gills like them fish, so they comes to the surface to breathe.'

He looked past me to the sea, and I turned to look. He seemed mesmerised by the water. Was he imagining the dolphins while he spoke?

'They're playful too,' he said. 'We often see 'em jumping out of the water. They comes and goes. You never knows when they gonna be here, but often they shows 'emselves early in the morning. Trouble is they disappear off once them holiday people arrive, making noises with all their swimming and splashing in the water.'

Joel looked thoughtful. 'Dolphins ... they're only one of hundreds of special sea animals round here. You only has to go into the shallow water and stand still ... even them tiny fish are special. Look down and you'll see them.

They comes right up and tickles your toes to make friends with you.'

'That sounds wonderful,' said Mum, 'we'll have to paddle, Lucy.'

My nose squidged up. I looked down towards the water's edge.

I'd always imagined the sea as a dangerous place. There was no way I was going to put my feet in there.

'Mmmm ... is it safe, Joel? Don't those creatures bite your toes?' I asked.

'You'll be fine, and if you swim and snorkel with a mask, you'll be seeing some wonderful creatures.'

Despite the heat, a shiver rippled through my body. Swim? Snorkel? No way.

'Ah, here they comes ... I been expectin' these two.' Joel was looking behind me. I turned to watch two boys walking towards us.

'This is young Solomon and Jack. They'll tell you how much fun they has in the water. I reckon they spends most of their spare time in the sea.'

Solomon and Jack seemed about my age. One boy was thin and tall, with bony knees. He was Caribbean with dark skin and short, black, curly hair. The other boy was a similar height to me and looked quite strong compared to his friend. His white skin was suntanned, and his straight fair hair was long enough to blow uncontrollably in the slight breeze. They both wore colourful shorts, with sleeveless tee shirts and their feet were in flip-flops.

'Hi, Grandpa.' The tall, skinny one spoke to Joel. 'Jack gave me a hand with the rest of the chairs, so we've finished early today.'

The tall boy turned and looked like he was going to speak to me, but he hesitated, and Jack beat him to it.

'G'day ... pleased to meet you. You on holiday here?' His accent made me frown. He was speaking English, but it didn't sound like he'd come from London.

Joel was looking my way. 'Jack and his parents ... they're Australian,' he explained. 'They've been here a couple of years. Came to start a new life, exactly like you're doing. Jack's Dad ... he runs the local garage.'

Joel quickly explained to the boys that we'd come to live in Jude's Bay, and Jack's immediate reaction was to whoop loudly. He looked straight at me.

'Hey, that's great, you can join Sol and me,' said Jack. 'We're always hanging out around the beach, swimming after school and you'll be coming on the bus to our school in St. Stephens, too. Yeah, it'll be cool. You'll soon feel at home here. I settled in pretty fast. We love it here and you can't beat the sea and all the swimming.'

I felt my body begin to shake. These two boys looked friendly enough and they wanted me to join in with their fun, but the very idea of going into the water scared me rigid. I couldn't swim. I certainly didn't want to learn. Perhaps they'd simply let me sit on the beach and watch while they played?

'It'd be perfect, Lucy, wouldn't it?' said Mum. 'If you spend time with Jack and Solomon you'll soon learn about those creatures in the sea.'

NO! The sea's dangerous! My fingers began twisting my hair and I looked at Mum, willing her to stop talking. But it got worse.

'Lucy doesn't know how to swim,' she told everyone, 'but I'm sure she'll soon learn.'

Why was Mum saying that? I didn't want everyone to know I couldn't swim.

I could never learn to swim. I'm scared of the water. Why didn't Mum realise that? I opened my mouth, then shut it again. What was the point in protesting anyway?

No-one ever listened to my point of view. My eyes were searching the faces around me. Why were they all ganging up on me? I don't want to go into the water. Why can't they leave me alone?

Joel was watching me. Perhaps he'd noticed I was uncomfortable with the suggestion of swimming? He banged both his hands on the table. 'Well, enough of this chatter. I'm getting hungry,' he said.

He suggested we stopped for a meal at Drifters and I listened as the conversation turned to Jack and Solomon's plans for the following day.

'We're going to do a beach clean-up,' said Jack. 'We try to clear up the rubbish before the wind blows it into the water of the bay. Plastic bottles and other stuff gets caught up in the rocks over there, too.' Jack pointed down the beach, then turned to me. 'You can come and help if you'd like. It's more fun than it might sound, honest!'

Mum was insistent that I help, so a time was set to meet the following morning.

'Great, we'll get some collection sacks and meet you here, okay?' Jack rubbed his hands, 'the more people that help the quicker it'll get done.'

Wonderful! Picking up litter! Probably the most boring thing I could think of doing. Still, at least they'd all stopped talking about me going in the water.

CHAPTER EIGHT

Beach Clean-up

The sun shone through a crack in my curtains. I looked at my watch. It wasn't time to get up yet.

I lay still. Memories of yesterday flooded back into my mind. Everyone had been wanting me to learn to swim. I shivered despite the warmth of the room.

I felt sick ... no, just breathe deeply, calm down ... logical thinking, that's what I should be doing. I didn't have to learn to swim if I didn't want to. I could say no!

It can't be that I'm worried about being in cold water ... the water can't be cold here in the hot Caribbean sun, so there's nothing to be frightened of ... stupid girl. Everyone must think me stupid, being so scared of the water.

I challenged myself to be brave and agree to learn to swim, but my bravery lasted only seconds before my doubts returned. It was all very well, everyone encouraging me to learn to swim, but I was scared. I didn't know what I was scared *of* ... drowning or ... being killed by a monster sea creature ... but I was certain I didn't want to go into the water.

My thoughts drifted back to London, at least I'd known the dangers there. I knew the risks of crossing the roads, full of busy traffic and the gangs of youths armed with knives who wandered around the estate where we lived. But here, on the island it seemed more frightening than London, with everything I'd not done or seen before ... it was all so scary. Here there was swimming and hurricanes

... and what were these boys really like? Would they be nasty to me like those girls in London? Would they be messing about and pushing me in the water? What was Mum doing, making me go and pick up rubbish with two boys I didn't even know?

I slowly got out of bed. Helping Solomon and Jack at the beach was certainly going to be different to what I was used to, but I wouldn't be texting back to my old friends in London and boasting I was just off collect rubbish! Images flashed through my brain of being pushed under the water ... or picking up a rusty tin can and cutting my hands. Hands covered in blood, yuk!

I made Mum a cup of tea. She rubbed her face as she woke.

'I slept very well. It's so quiet here.' She yawned, noisily. 'I'm really pleased you agreed to do the beach clean-up today. You'll get to know Jack and Solomon a bit better too. They were so polite, and it'll be great for you to help them. Have a wonderful time!'

I would go and I'd be helpful, but that didn't mean I was going to enjoy it!

'Yeah, see you later. Bye!'

As I walked onto the beach, I could see the boys outside Drifters.

'Hi, Lucy,' said Solomon. He held a baseball cap towards me. 'You'll need a sunhat ... you can borrow this.'

He passed me a scruffy cap with 'Gone Fishing' written across the top. It was a gruesome, sun-bleached brown colour. 'I didn't think you'd be kitted up with hot weather stuff yet.'

'You're right, I haven't got a sun hat, thanks,' I said. I stared at the tatty old cap ... I would never have chosen to wear anything so awful. It was faded, torn, and felt sticky, I couldn't stop my face screwing up in disgust.

'It's okay,' said Solomon, 'it's just a bit old and might have a bit of salt on it from where it's been worn on one of the boats. Salt gets sticky when its dried. It won't hurt you, though.'

It was only eight o'clock, but the sun was already hot, so I pulled the hat on, tucking my long hair through the hole at the back. I hoped no-one would recognise me. Stupid girl! There's no-one here who knows me anyway. None of my friends were here.

My eyes suddenly felt damp and I wiped away a couple of tears. Don't show these two boys you're upset ... be strong! Luckily, they were sorting out the rubbish collection bags and not looking at me.

I was wearing my old dark-blue shorts and a plain white tee shirt that'd been part of my school uniform in London. I hoped I didn't look too out of place, as everyone I'd seen on Pontus so far had been wearing colourful clothes. Jack and Sol both had colourful tee shirts and knee-length shorts, but they also looked quite scruffy.

Jack saw me looking at the ripped pocket of his shorts.

'Yeah, okay.' He shrugged. 'I got caught up with the door handle of the shed where Sol keeps the beach chairs, but they'll do for collecting rubbish. I expect once you've been shopping and spent all your Mum's money, you'll be looking like a fashion model.'

'Won't look smart for long if she hangs around with us,' said Sol. When he smiled, he showed a mouthful of very white teeth.

'Yep, you'll soon get salt-stained and scruffy from messing around in the sea, and end up looking exactly like Sol and me,' said Jack. He started laughing, and Sol joined in.

Mmmm, they're still keen to get me swimming then.

I looked at the rubbish collection bags Jack was sorting out, then glanced around. The edge of the beach by the road was scruffy with weeds and overgrown grass, and amongst the trees, by the footpath, there was loads of discarded rubbish. I remembered the gardens on our journey from the airport ... lots of those had looked like waste tips too. I looked along the beach but couldn't see what I was searching for. At home, there were special rubbish areas on the ground level of our block of flats for recycling paper and plastic, and there were bins in the High Street. Although the bins overflowed sometimes, and dustmen dropped some of the litter on collection days, most of the time it was kept tidy, but here, I couldn't see any bins at all. Where were they? Did people just throw their rubbish on the ground? How strange!

'I wonder how much stuff we'll pick up today?' said Jack, 'we could have a bag each and have a competition.'

'No,' said Solomon, 'we shouldn't race over those rocks, it'll be too easy to fall and break an ankle.'

'Typical! Sol, you always think about keeping safe all the time,' said Jack.

'Probably cos I'm SO lucky.' Sol smiled at me as he explained. 'I've got a little brother, who's just four and baby twin sisters. I'm always having to help look after them. It gets to be a habit to think about safety.'

'So, you're looking after me like a four-year old, eh! Thanks,' said Jack, laughing. 'Anyhow, whatever rubbish we get will be great. I expect the three of us will be able to collect a lot this morning.'

'We try to collect rubbish before it blows into the sea,' explained Sol, 'and Grandpa bought these collection bags specially - they're made of starch or something - so they're not plastic bags.'

I took a closer look. They looked like ordinary plastic dustbin bags to me, large, black and slippery. Strangely though, they smelt a bit like carrots and raw potatoes.

'Yeah,' said Jack, 'when plastic gets into the ocean it can harm the sea creatures.'

'It's a good idea to keep the beach tidy,' I said, 'it's beautiful here, but won't people just drop more litter again? I can't see any rubbish bins anywhere. People seem to have dropped rubbish all over the place. Surely, you're both wasting your time if people aren't encouraged to use bins.'

'We're just trying to stop it all going into the sea,' said Jack, glaring at me.'

Perhaps I should have kept my thoughts to myself.

'I guess everything is new to you here, isn't it?' said Jack. 'Perhaps you should talk to Joel later.'

'He'll explain it better than us,' said Sol. 'He'll help you understand how we live on the island. It's bound to be different from where you've come from.'

'He'll tell you all about sea creatures too,' said Jack, smiling again. 'I've learned loads from him.'

Mmmm. Mum had been listening carefully to Joel last night and I suppose he did seem to know a lot, but I still wasn't sure about him ... and now ... picking up litter just seemed a total waste of time!

Jack handed out a bag to each of us and tried to tuck the spare bags into what was left of the pocket of his shorts, then decided to loop them all through his belt.

'At school last year, we did a space project,' said Solomon, 'and I learnt that the astronauts left a load of rubbish on the moon. If we don't pick up our litter, then our whole planet will end up looking like a rubbish tip here on Earth too.'

'Good point, Sol! Everyone ready?' asked Jack. He marched off ahead of us ... stretching one arm in the air. 'Let's go and save the world!'

Mmmm - save the world? What was he talking about? How could just the three of us make a difference?

CHAPTER NINE

The Edge of the Sea

I'd never walked close to the edge of the sea before. I watched as surf gently bubbled up the beach, then got sucked back into the sea. As each fresh wave came up, the water smoothed and flattened the sand. I couldn't imagine any danger in learning to swim if it stayed calm like this. Surely, I could try to learn to swim in these peaceful conditions.

As we walked and collected rubbish, Solomon explained that Joel owned all the chairs and umbrellas on Dolphin Beach.

'I help my Grandpa every morning by putting out chairs and after school I bring 'em all in again. Sometimes Jack helps in the afternoon, then I can finish early, and we have more time to swim or snorkel.'

'What time were you up this morning?' I asked, looking at all the beach furniture neatly stretched out across the beach.

'Six o'clock. That's normal for me. Once the sun starts shining, I can't sleep, so I go and put the beach chairs out. Gramps collects the hire money from the people on holiday, during the day.'

'That sounds like abuse of child labour to me,' I said, grumpily. 'Nobody would be asking children in London to get up early every morning and work before school. I think we stopped children going up chimneys in London, over a hundred years ago!'

'No-one makes me do it,' said Sol, quietly. 'I just do it to help my Grandpa.'

We walked for a while in silence.

As I looked around, I couldn't seem to lose my grumpy mood. The beach might be beautiful, but it wasn't my home ... and life here was so different. Lots of tumble-down houses, hurricanes, and now children working all hours of the day ... it was poles apart from my old life in London.

Jack's voice disturbed my thoughts. When I realised he was asking questions about London I let my grumpiness seep away and chatted about where I'd lived. As we talked, we also collected plastic bottles, bits of rubber flip-flops, broken pieces of polystyrene packaging, coffee cups and some discarded bits of fishing line.

Jack had wandered ahead when I saw pieces of orange peel floating in the water near to the edge. I decided to be brave and try to reach it. I planted my feet in, hoping there wouldn't be any sea monsters waiting to bite my toes.

I breathed deeply and walked slowly into the sea. It was shallow and as the sun shone through the surface, I could see the sand below. Compared to the heat of the sun, the water felt chilly around my ankles.

One step. Two steps. As I reached down to pick up the peel, the sand moved from under my feet. My whole body jolted. I lost my balance! I was going to fall over. I turned and raced towards the beach, water splashing everywhere. My imagination took over ... the sea was trying to eat me, and sea monsters were waiting to snap at my ankles. There was a whole personal disaster movie going on in my head.

My legs pulled my knees towards my chin as I took each foot higher and higher out of the water, desperately heading for Solomon and the safety of the sandy beach. I could hear someone squealing, then realised it was me.

'Well done,' said Solomon, smiling. 'Was that your first time in the water?'

'Yep, I thought there was a monster fish lurking ... waiting to attack me.'

'Did something happen to you to make you scared of water, Lucy?' Sol asked.

'No, I don't think so,' I said, 'and it's not those little waves that frighten me. I think it's my imagination. It's the thought of being surrounded by deep, dark water and not being able to see if there's something dangerous in there. But I'm also rubbish when I wash my hair or have a shower too, as I can't bear to get water in my eyes.'

'You'll be fine,' said Solomon. 'Take it gently and we'll help you get used to everything. All this must be really strange for you.' He smiled again, but this time his eyes were looking down at the sand.

'I'll look after you,' he said quietly.

We'd been collecting rubbish for over an hour, but I couldn't get enthusiastic about helping. Jack and Sol were keen to pick up everything, but I kept thinking that even if we picked up all the rubbish we could see, by tomorrow the beach would probably be covered in a whole load more of new stuff.

We were close to the rocks when I saw it. A large, black shape on the sand.

'What's that?' I asked.

We ran towards it. 'It's a turtle,' yelled Jack, as we got closer. 'That's strange. They usually only come ashore when they need to lay eggs and that's not for months yet. I've no idea what it's doing on the beach now.'

'Perhaps we should try to push it back into the water,' said Sol. 'It must've beached itself. Perhaps it got lost.'

'It's a hawksbill turtle. Look at its sharp, beaky mouth,' said Jack.

41

Solomon looked worried. 'It's in danger here,' he said. 'Turtles are supposed to live in the sea, not sit on a beach in the heat of the sun.'

It was a big turtle. I estimated it was nearly half a metre long and maybe thirty centimetres in height at the top of the rounded, heavy shell which was the tallest part of its body. It wasn't moving and its eyes were closed.

I bent down close to its head and whispered. 'Hey turtle, what's your problem? Do you need some help? Why aren't you going back into the sea?'

There was no response. It was so still. I hoped it was asleep and not in serious trouble. My breathing became faster and deep inside my brain there was a bell ringing ... an emergency bell. I wanted to help this creature. I couldn't leave it here to die. But how could we help ... and had we arrived in time?

CHAPTER TEN

Turtle in Trouble

Gently touching the top of its scaly head made the turtle open its eyes. Phew! At least the poor creature was still alive.

I looked into the turtle's eye. It looked back at me. I got closer and spoke quietly. 'Are you asking me for help? Yes, of course, I'll help you.'

The turtle suddenly blinked. 'Did you understood what I said?' I looked up at Sol and Jack, 'I think it trusts us to help it.'

It moved its mouth closer to my face. No ... don't kiss me. I pulled away. I didn't fancy a kiss from its sharp, beaky mouth.

It kept opening its mouth.

'It seems to be trying to show me something.' I looked inside its mouth and my heart stopped. I saw a blue plastic grocery bag.

Solomon leaned closer. 'Grandpa told me last week that plastic bags look just like underwater jellyfish, when they're full of water and drifting in the current,' he said, 'and jellyfish are a turtle's favourite food. It must've mistaken the plastic bag for a tasty bit of food and swallowed it. I can't believe I'm seeing exactly what Gramps was telling me about.'

I realised now why Jack and Solomon were trying to stop plastic rubbish from being swept into the sea. Poor turtle. I had to help this amazing animal.

'Jack, can you help me here? Try to hold the turtle's head up. That's it ... and Sol, can you force the turtle's jaw open? I can't keep the mouth open at the same time as I put my hand inside.'

Both boys were eager to help and the three of us surrounded the turtle. I couldn't see any teeth, but the beak and hard gums looked like they would take my fingers off if it closed its mouth suddenly. Our eyes meet again. It's okay. I'll try and get it out for you. I communicated by thought.

There was a tear at the corner of its eye. The turtle blinked the moisture away, looked straight at me and kept its mouth wide open. Was it reading my thoughts when we looked at each other?

'Keep your mouth open,' I whispered, 'keep still.

I grabbed hold of the plastic and pulled. There was a lot of it, as the bag wasn't only in its mouth, it was also disappearing down the back of the turtle's throat.

It was wet and slippery and hard to get hold of, but slowly the bag started to slide towards me. Then the turtle coughed and gurgled, shaking its head. Was the bag hurting its throat?

Hey, mind you don't bite my fingers off! I pulled my hand out of its mouth fast, just as it closed. Phew! I thought you were going to bite me then. Are you okay now? Can I try again? Again, the turtle seemed to calm down as I silently passed my thoughts across to it. The turtle blinked at me, so I reached in, grasped the bag and pulled. Slowly the plastic bag came towards me.

'Yeah, that's it, Lucy, you're doing it.' said Sol. The bag slid out of the turtle's mouth.

'It's probably not had anything to eat since it swallowed the bag.' said Jack. 'It must be starving.'

I pushed the slimy plastic bag deep into the rubbish collection bag. I didn't want it taken by the breeze, back into the sea, for the same thing to happen to another turtle.

'It must need food,' said Jack. 'We'll have to carry or push it back to the water. We need to get it out of the hot sun soon.'

Jack and Sol stood at either side and tried to lift the turtle, but they really struggled. 'I don't think we can lift it,' said Sol, 'it weighs far too much.'

'Why don't we use the spare rubbish bags,' I suggested. Both boys looked at me, frowning.

'I remember once when it snowed in England,' I explained. 'People made sledges out of some plastic bags to slide down a hill. I think we could use the same system. The slippery bags could help us slide the turtle over the sand.'

'What can I do?' asked Sol.

'Lift the turtle up a little bit and I'll push some bags underneath. Then we'll pull the bags to the water with the turtle on top.'

'Hey,' yelled Jack, 'great idea.'

Within seconds we were working as a team. Sol and Jack lifted a large front flipper up high enough for me to push a bag underneath. Then we did the same for the other side, so each flipper was now sitting on a slippery rubbish sack. We did the same to the smaller back legs.

We rushed to the front of the turtle. It was facing up the beach, so first, we had to turn it around before we could pull it into the sea.

'Okay, are we ready?' My hands were shaking. What if my idea didn't work?

With Jack on one side of the turtle and Sol and me on the other, we dragged the bags enough to spin the turtle around to face the sea. Then we walked backwards, pulling together and headed for the water.

'That's it! It's moving! Here we go!' said Jack.

The animal was heavy, but the bags provided a perfect surface on which to slide the turtle over the sand.

We splashed into the water and as the water got deeper the turtle began to float. Jack collected all the bags as they slipped away from underneath its body. Then, the turtle moved its flippers by itself. As the water got deeper, it started to swim.

'Off you go, back into the wild ocean,' I said.

The turtle began to head away, then turned and came back. It nuzzled against my knee.

Down through the water I could see its eye. It blinked slowly. Was it saying goodbye? Or thank you?

It turned and began to swim away using its powerful flippers. The water supported its weight, so it swam easily. It was back in its special watery world, heading out to the deep sea. It was such a beautiful animal.

'Of course, you must be hungry!' I said. 'I hope you'll find some real jellyfish to eat. They'd be much tastier than a plastic bag!'

'Hey Lucy, you're in quite deep water,' Jack shouted. 'Go carefully. Don't fall over.'

I looked down. I couldn't see my knees. Water surrounded me; it was halfway up my thighs. My legs had disappeared.

I was so far away from the beach. What if I slipped? What if my face ended up in the water? I clenched my hands into fists, willing my legs to keep me standing upright. My eyes were misting with tears.

'Give me your hand,' said Sol. He'd come back into the water to stand beside me and was reaching out towards me.

Turning to face the beach I grabbed Sol's hand. He kept me steady as my feet got used to walking on the wet, moving sand. Slowly, we shuffled back to the beach.

'Brilliant, Luce,' said Jack. 'I can't believe we just did that! Don't worry about the water, you'll get used to it soon.'

Soon? I don't think it's as easy for me as that, Jack. I was shaking and shivering.

Stamping my feet on the solid sand I realised I was safe, but what about my friend, the turtle? How safe was it for the turtle swimming in the ocean?

I'd felt a special connection with the turtle when we'd looked at each other. Had it been trying to tell me something? Was it asking me to help? Did it want me to protect all the turtles from the plastic in the sea?

Perhaps I could learn more about their lives and the dangers threatening them. Maybe I could help to protect them?

'I'll start as soon as I can,' I whispered, 'I'll help you ... I promise.'

CHAPTER ELEVEN

Telling the Tale

We headed for the rocks. There was litter in every crevice and Sol was right about the danger. The rocks were wet from sea spray, and I had to concentrate to find a way across without slithering and trapping an ankle.

Most of the rubbish was plastic ... straws, bags and loads of water bottles. Just how much of this litter went into the ocean? What damage was it doing?

'I'm going to ask Joel about the dangers of litter in the ocean,' I said.

'Well, we've never seen a turtle in trouble like that on the beach before, and we don't see much of what's going on beneath the surface of the ocean. It's probably best to talk to Joel,' said Jack. 'Yeah, Joel will have the answers, he knows everything about the sea.'

When we'd filled two big bags each, we dragged them across the sand to the back of Drifters Restaurant. We closed the tops, tying them tightly to stop the wind blowing the rubbish out again.

'How often do we need to do a beach clean, Sol?' I asked. 'Without any bins where do people put their rubbish? Will the beach be full of litter again tomorrow?'

'There always seems to be rubbish, but perhaps we can get Grandpa to talk to people as he takes the money for the chair hire?' said Sol. 'Ask them to make sure to take their litter home with them. That'd help.'

'Well, that's okay if they're trying to not leave it around but there must be stuff that just blows in from other places.' I said. 'Perhaps we should work as a team when you collect the chairs back in. Between us we can try to keep the beach clean.'

'What's that, are you volunteering me to help every day? asked Jack.

'Well, we need to look after the turtles, don't we?' I said. 'Perhaps if Joel speaks to people there may not be too much to collect and then perhaps, we could do it every other day.'

'That sounds better,' said Jack. 'Okay, we'll trial that tomorrow.'

'Well done, you three,' said a voice I recognised. Joel was coming out of the shed behind us. 'Six bags, fantastic work!'

Jack's voice was loud and excited as he explained our turtle rescue.

'... it was down to Lucy that we got the turtle back into the water. It was her idea to pull it over the sand, and that saved its life. We'd never have been able to lift it.'

Joel turned towards me, grinning so widely that he showed all the gaps in his teeth.

'Well, what a heroine you are,' said Joel, fingering his stubbly, white beard. 'I've heard some stories in my time, but today you proved to be a very special young lady. To save a magnificent creature like a turtle ... girl, you should be real proud of yourself.'

He was smiling, and his crinkly brown eyes were sparkling at me.

I beamed. Perhaps this old man wasn't so bad after all.

Sol had listened to his grandpa praising my rescue of the turtle. He turned and we exchanged a high-five.

'Trouble is, Sol,' I said, 'there must be loads more plastic out there and other turtles making the same mistakes, thinking the bags are jellyfish. It's probably happening right now while we're standing here talking about it. There must be something more we can do.'

Sol frowned. 'Yeah, but what?'

'We need people to understand what's happening,' I said. 'I'm sure the turtle was looking at me and asking for help. I can't just sit back and do nothing.'

Our conversation was interrupted when Mum arrived.

Joel gave his speech all over again.

'That turtle would've died for certain if young Lucy hadn't helped it.' Joel couldn't stop talking about my adventure. 'Yep, he'd have been a gonna for sure.' Joel looked at Mum. 'It's great having you and Lucy living here.'

Mum smiled and put her arm around my shoulders to squeeze me tight, then bought us cool drinks at Drifters Bar.

'It wasn't just me, Mum,' I explained. 'I couldn't have rescued it without Jack and Sol ... we worked as a team to get it back into the water.'

'Well, I'm proud of you all. You've done something really good today and while you've been busy saving turtles,' she said, 'I popped into St. Stephens on the bus. The market was fabulous. There's so much to choose from.'

'Did you get me anything?' I asked.

'I certainly did!' said Mum, 'I got your school uniform sorted and also bought white shorts, coloured tee shirts and proper beach sandals. Will that suit you, m'lady?' Giggling, she bowed as if she were serving a Queen.

'Great.' I gave Mum a hug. 'That'll be better than my old school sports kit.'

I looked at Joel and realised the worries I'd had about him were fading. I leaned closer to him, speaking quietly.

'Joel? This might sound a bit strange, but when I looked into the turtle's eye, it felt like it was talking to me. Does that sound silly?'

'Silly? Absolutely not,' he said. 'It sounds perfect. Communicating through the eye of a turtle can change your life, young Lucy. That's a gift, that is. A real gift. It means you can understand and get close to these animals. Yeah, I reckon you got it alright!'

'Can you help me to understand the sea creatures, Joel? I really want to help protect them and get other people to look after them, too. It doesn't seem fair that litter is getting into their world.'

'Well, of course, I can help you learn about the animals, Lucy,' he said, 'but the best thing you can do is to learn to swim and even learn to dive. Then you'll be able to look around underwater and begin to understand the special world where all these creatures live.'

'No way. I couldn't do that. Have you seen how scared I am of water?'

Joel raised his eyebrows and smiled.

'Yeah, okay,' I said, 'I understand what you're saying … about how great it would be down there looking at the sea life, but ... but it's totally terrifying ... how can I do it, when I'm so frightened of the water?'

'I'm sure you'll be wanting to swim as soon as possible.' Joel was still smiling. 'Once you understand the sea, it'll change your life, Lucy. I can see you becoming a real wildlife expert as you grow older, and I'm certain you're brave enough. You'll get over your fear of the water, trust me, I know you can do it.'

I smiled back. Was Joel right?

Mum's voice interrupted my worries.

'Oh, I meant to say, I also bought you a swimsuit patterned with blue and green fish.' said Mum, 'so you can learn to swim.'

I'd started to get used to the idea of trying to be brave about water, but … Mum buying me a swimsuit ... getting my whole body in the water ... noooooooooooooooo! How scary was that?

'If you've got a swimsuit now, then let's get you into the water this afternoon,' said Jack. 'Sol and I'll be with you all the time. We'll look after you, honest!'

Sol was nodding too. 'Come on Lucy, you'll get used to it sooner than you think, you'll enjoy it.'

Everyone was looking at me.

'Start by getting your toes wet, then a little bit more ... I knows you can do it, gradual like, bit at a time.' said Joel. 'No rush, but the sooner you can swim, then the sooner you'll be able to help them sea creatures.'

I thought of the turtle and knew I was going to have to face up to this challenge. They needed help and if I could get used to the water, perhaps I could help them?

'Okay,' I said. Was that really my voice? Did I just say that? What was I letting myself in for?

The afternoon turned into a whole load of scary moments. Of course, I started out scared and squealing, but Jack and Sol were so kind to me. It wasn't long before I stopped being totally scared and began to enjoy myself. We laughed all afternoon, but they never laughed AT me. They never made me feel silly because I was scared.

Sol borrowed some arm bands to help me float.

'I'm gonna look like a two-year old now,' I said.

'Doesn't matter ... you only need them to begin with, just to make you feel confident,' said Sol. 'Anyway, it's only us here. No-one's looking at you.'

Jack found a beach ball in Joel's shed and we messed about in the water for ages, always staying shallow enough for my feet to still touch the seabed.

I even tried a few swimming strokes. I was useless, but I actually got my shoulders under the water. Was this me? Was I actually doing this?

It got cooler as the sun began to dip, so we reluctantly walked back up the beach to where Joel and Mum were sitting at a long Drifters' picnic table. Mum lined up some fizzy drinks for us and we dried off.

'Well, Lucy,' Joel was smiling at me. 'Did you see any sea monsters this afternoon?'

'No ... but I guess all that splashing around frightened them off. I expect they're hiding in the deep water, where we can't see them.'

Joel rolled his eyes upwards and his head shook with laughter.

I turned away, so Joel couldn't see that I was giggling too, but I wasn't quite ready to admit those scary monsters might only be in my imagination.

CHAPTER TWELVE

Scared of a Fish?

'There's someone you need to meet,' said Joel, looking across Drifters Bar.

'That's Dan, he owns the Dive Centre up by the road.' A tall, fair-haired, untidy man had stopped at the bar to chat with the waitress.

'He's been teaching today,' said Joel. 'Those'll be his students.' He pointed to six young men, standing in a circle, noisily discussing their day. 'I guess they's finished their dive training for the day.'

When the young divers heard Mum's English accent, they started chatting to us.

'You mean, you're not on holiday? You actually live here?' one asked. 'Hey, that's amazing!'

'Yeah, that's cool,' said another. 'The reefs are great. I suppose you get to dive here all the time?'

I didn't get a chance to say I couldn't dive before I heard another diver speaking.

'I got too close to a crack in the coral this afternoon, where a moray eel was hiding. It's a skinny, slithery fish, with a mouthful of sharp teeth ... and it really made me jump,' he said. 'It came charging out of the crevice. I thought it was gonna bite me.'

'Scared of a fish, eh, Jamie?' another diver teased.

'I had a right to be scared,' said Jamie. 'That fish had enormous teeth!'

All the divers were laughing when one of them came up behind Jamie and shouted 'BOO' which made Jamie jump and they laughed even more.

'We've not been on the Island long enough to learn to dive,' said Mum, speaking to the first diver.

'Well, get Dan to teach you. He's brilliant,' said Jamie.

'Yeah, he's not so bad for an old bloke,' said one diver.

'Yep, he must be at least thirty!' said another, laughing.

'He knows his stuff though and you always feel safe with him,' said Jamie.

I looked towards Dan.

'Well, I know they all like him,' I whispered, 'but he looks scruffier than anyone I've seen on the Island so far. He's like one of those beggars we used to see on the streets of London. He's got a half-grown dirty beard; his hair is a tangled mess and he looks like he's slept in his clothes!'

'Joel looks pretty scruffy too, but he's someone I trust,' said Mum.

'Ummm … you're probably right about Joel but I'm not sure Dan is very pleasant at all,' I said, 'if he can't even be bothered to be clean and tidy.'

Looking away from Dan, Mum pulled on my sleeve to stop me talking about him.

'We shouldn't be talking about people out loud, Lucy,' said Mum. 'Remember, Joel's encouraged us to meet him, so Dan must be alright.'

Although I'd begun to trust Joel's opinions, I wasn't sure I could get to like Dan. I glared at him grumpily.

'Don't stare at him like that,' Mum said. 'I'm sure he's okay really. Don't make a decision about him until we've at least spoken to him. I've loved listening to those divers. They must know him well and they seem to think he's a good instructor.'

'Maybe,' I muttered.

As Dan moved away from the bar, Joel grabbed his arm and brought him over.

'Come to live here? That's great,' said Dan. 'So how long have you been here? ... whereabouts are you living? ... how are you settling in?'

When Joel told Dan about the turtle rescue, Dan turned towards me. His face had broken into a really big grin.

'That's marvellous! Great you could think so quickly and sensibly. That was a perfect solution! Yep, I agree with Joel. Well done, Lucy.'

Then he looked quizzically at me.

'Do you need a part-time job after school, Lucy?' he asked. He was smiling at me across the table where we'd all sat down.

'Really,' I said, 'you don't even know me.' His smile seemed quite warm, but I wasn't at all sure I wanted to work for this untidy man, whose hair was thick with salt and tied back from his face with a piece of old string.

'It depends on what you're expecting her to do,' said Mum. Maybe she wasn't so convinced about him after all? She'd seemed happy to accept him as a scruffy and unkempt character but asking me to work for him seemed to be one step too far. I realised she'd gone into motherly protection mode. She put her shoulders back and sat up straight, shaking her body like a bird rustling its feathers. Mum was turning into a parrot right in front of my eyes.

'It's important for Lucy to settle into school first,' squawked Mum, 'and for us both to find our way in these new surroundings.'

'It's okay,' said Dan, 'I'll look after her. I just need some sensible help with the Dive Centre, and Lucy showed us this morning that she's quick-thinking and practical. She'd be perfect.'

Dan grinned at me even more. I started to change my mind about him. Perhaps he wasn't so bad as I originally thought. He seemed different to what I'd first imagined and was very complimentary about my efforts with the turtle rescue. I started to smile, but Mum glared at me with beady, bird-like eyes. We seemed to have swopped sides ... although I'd got over Dan's initial scruffiness ... Mum now seemed suspicious of him.

I frowned, hoping the bird-like Mum wouldn't stop me hearing about what might be, an exciting job.

'So, can you dive, Lucy?' he asked.

'Well, no,' I said, looking down at my feet. 'Actually, I can't even swim properly yet.'

'I've got an idea, let me show you both the Dive Centre,' Dan suggested. 'I've got a small pool out the back, where I can teach you to swim.'

A job after school sounded a good idea, but should I tell him how rubbish I was at swimming, or how I panicked so easily?

We followed Dan to the Dive Centre, walking along the beach to the narrow path, then threading our way through a few parked cars. Mum was still mumbling to herself about settling in first.

In front of us was a huge, colourful building with the main entrance to the Dive Centre at the front on the road side and a small shop called 'The Beach Shack', facing out towards the beach at the back. There were signs with big letters, 'Neptune Dive Centre' and windows with posters of divers swimming underwater.

Whilst Dan was unlocking the front door, Mum pulled me to one side.

'Look, Lucy, I want us to make friends and meet people, of course I do, but this man looks lazy. He doesn't bother with his appearance even though he's running a business. It's probably not even a proper business. If you're going to get an after-school job, we've got to make sure it's not with some sort of rogue who's expecting you to do all the work while he sits with his feet up.'

I pulled at Mum's arm and put a finger over my lips. 'Ssshh ... let's look around before we decide.' I said, quietly.

I sort of understood what Mum was worried about, but for some reason, I wasn't concerned. Yes, Dan did look like some sort of outrageous pirate, but did that mean we couldn't trust him? He seemed a warm and kind sort of person. But, was Mum right? Was my decision about Dan being taken too fast? Was he safe?

The questioning in my head leapt to stories about stranger danger. Surely, I wouldn't have considered doing this back in London ... he seemed kind beneath the untidiness, but I wasn't completely sure I could trust him.

CHAPTER THIRTEEN

Neptune Dive Centre

When we walked into the Dive Centre, I thought it had been burgled. It was a total mess, with everything thrown over the floor and strange looking equipment stacked haphazardly on shelves.

'That must be diving kit,' said Mum, 'those are fins and masks. I've seen them on TV.'

There were piles of paper spread across the reception desk, with more on the floor behind it. Cardboard boxes, with their contents half-emptied, were tucked under shelves. There were boxes containing tee shirts printed with cartoons of laughing sharks; baseball hats of varying colours; fish identification cards and dive logbooks, but it all needed to be displayed properly.

'I know I'm a bit untidy,' said Dan.

Untidy? No! It was much more than that ... this was chaos!

Dan turned and saw Mum's frown.

'Yeah, it's a bit of a clutter, but I've been busy teaching people to dive all this week and there doesn't seem enough time in the day to do it all. But it does get better,' explained Dan. 'Come and have a look out the back. I always make sure my students respect the diving equipment.'

We walked through to the equipment room, which at first glance looked as chaotic as the reception desk, but then I saw loads of rubbery wetsuits hanging up neatly.

There was a separate area with a notice 'Generator Room', where air tanks were lined up smartly with special numbers around the top.

'This looks a bit better,' Mum whispered.

'Perhaps the mess is why he needs help,' I whispered back.

Dan took us out to the beach at the back of the Centre.

'I built all this last March,' he said.

There was a smart, paved patio area around a swimming pool, with sunloungers, straw umbrellas and wooden picnic tables. A shower and toilet block had been built to one side, painted white, with a typical Caribbean roof of red corrugated iron.

'I start the beginner's dive course in the pool out here,' Dan explained. 'It's important to build the divers' confidence with their equipment whilst they are in the safety of the pool, before they go out into the sea.'

Mum was nodding. 'Good to know he's looking after people's safety,' she whispered.

Dan looked at me. 'Would you like to use this pool after school, Lucy?'

I looked at the pool. At least the water was clear. I couldn't imagine any creepy sea creatures in there, but I wasn't sure I could ever learn to swim properly.

Go on. Be brave. You can do it.

Who said that? I seemed to be talking to myself. Perhaps my brain was trying to be positive, but I didn't know where my brain was getting the encouragement from. The inner voice was interrupted by Dan.

'I'll give you some lessons,' he said, 'and you'll soon be swimming around like a fish. I love getting people to be happy in the water.' Then he turned to Mum. 'Do you swim, Sarah? You could learn too!'

Mum smiled nervously and looked away. She'd never learnt to swim either.

Dan didn't wait for Mum's answer before he explained he'd like me to keep his Dive Centre tidy. He also suggested I could help restock the shelves in The Beach Shack.

'I definitely need someone sensible to help in there,' Dan said, 'so if you could come in for an hour after school, that would be perfect. I employ a regular shop assistant, Rene, who works during the day. She's a local nineteen-year-old who never stops laughing and all the children who come in for ice cream love her. You'll get on well with her.'

I looked at the untidiness of the place but was sure I could sort it out quite quickly. It wouldn't be hard work for me as I loved organizing things, and it sounded exciting.

'Most mornings,' Dan continued, 'I take visiting divers out to the local coral reef, then do paperwork in the afternoon,' he said, 'but sometimes the folks on holiday here only have one or two days to learn to dive, so I spend the whole day with them, teaching and getting them their first qualification to dive safely.'

Mum was nodding and smiling too. The parrot-like Mum had flown away, and she'd returned to normal.

'Okay,' she whispered, 'maybe I was wrong. Perhaps he's not the work-shy, lay-about I thought he was, even though he's still very scruffy! Rene sounds friendly too.'

'What do you think about the idea?' Dan asked. He looked first at me and then at Mum.

'Well, if Lucy's happy, it would be excellent for her to come here after school, while I'm still at work,' said Mum, 'and it would be great if you teach her to swim properly.'

'I'm happy to help in the Dive Centre,' I said, quickly, 'but I'm useless at swimming. I'm still a bit panicky.'

'You'll be fine,' he said, 'we'll take it slowly.'

We walked back to the reception area and Dan gave me a white baseball cap with 'Neptune Dive Centre' written across the front. I pushed my hair through the back of the cap and pulled it on. This was much better than Sol's scruffy old fishing hat.

Dan smiled. 'Right then, Lucy, welcome to the Neptune Dive Centre team. I think we'll get along fine. Well, that's two people who I've employed today. I'm trying out a young local chap too, he can dive quite well, so he'll be useful to me in the mornings when I'm taking divers out. His name's Bradley. I expect you'll get on fine, and once you've mastered swimming, I can teach you to dive too? I've taught Jack and Solomon and they love it. Then you'd be useful to me at weekends. You could come out and help my students on the dive boat. I can't pay you, but I can teach you to dive. Dive students usually give the helpers on the boat some money, so when you're on the boat, you can keep that money for yourself.'

Now he was talking about teaching me to dive. No! Jamie the diver had just told us about how he'd been attacked by a moray eel. I couldn't possibly go underwater if there were dangerous creatures there. Then the inner voice spoke up again. Go for it... you'll be okay ... be brave.

When Joel heard that I had got a job in the Dive Centre with Dan, he chortled, and his body shook as he laughed.

'Yeah, that Dan ... he's a good judge of character,' he said. 'Trust him to snap you up. I reckon you'll enjoy every minute working with him, and he's gonna teach you to swim proper, too. That's a real, good deal.'

'Yep. He's running the Pontus Island child labour system too,' I said, smiling, 'same as Sol does working for you in the mornings. Dan's got me working for no pay ... but says he'll teach me to dive, though.'

'Hey, that's a great bargain, that is,' said Joel, 'you gonna be ready to help them sea creatures proper then.'

CHAPTER FOURTEEN

St. Stephens School

Mum came with me on my first school day to do all the paperwork, so we got on the bus with Jack and Solomon to travel into St. Stephens. The boys wished me good luck and walked off to their classrooms, whilst Mum and I sat in the corridor outside the school office and waited to talk to the school secretary about the entry forms and give her information from my previous school.

'Well, this looks good,' said Mum, 'the building looks colourful and sturdy' I bit my tongue. I wasn't going to mention hurricanes today. I was too busy wondering if I would make friends with anyone.

'There must be a school assembly going to start,' I said. Pupils were coming from all directions towards a school hall. I began to look down at my feet, but it was soon obvious that I didn't have to worry. As lines of girls and boys passed me, a number of children said 'Hi.' Some smiled and some younger girls even waved at me, just moving their hands at the wrists as they walked past with cheeky grins on their faces. Everyone seemed friendly. 'This would never have happened in my old school,' I said to Mum, 'I think they would all have ignored us.'

'They do seem friendly and they're all so smart in their uniforms too,' she said.

When all the children had gone into the hall, we heard singing.

The paperwork was soon sorted and when assembly was over my new form teacher, Mrs. Willis, came past the office to collect me. She seemed even younger than my Mum. She was dressed in a colourful loose dress and sandals. She had glossy black, perfect skin and wavy black hair.

'Well,' she said, looking at the form which we'd filled out. 'We're very privileged to have you join our school. It looks like you're going to fit really well into my class. All my children work hard, so you're going to enjoy coming here.'

I relaxed, and smiled back at the warm, friendly woman who was speaking to me. Trouble was, I'd no idea how my classmates were going to react to me.

Mum collected all the lists of information including school holiday dates and left to go to her new job at the Community Library. 'Have a good day, Lucy. I'll see you later ... Jack and Solomon have promised to make sure you get the right bus home.'

Mrs Willis walked me down to her classroom. There was nothing sinister there. Nothing for me to worry about. The room had colourful wall art everywhere and was full of books. This was so much more welcoming than the dismal grey-walled secondary school I'd attended in London.

'All our pupils have tablets to work on too,' Mrs Willis explained, 'to improve their computing skills.' As she spoke her pupils arrived back from the hall and I was introduced to the class. So many of them were excited ... excited to have someone new in their class; someone from another country; someone with different coloured skin. The room was buzzing, and the warmth of their welcome made me smile. Then I saw I wasn't alone, there was another white girl in the class. 'Emily,' called Mrs Willis, 'I'd like you to look after Lucy until she can find her way around the school. She's on the same timetable for lessons as you, so it'll be easy for you. Look after her at lunchtime too and bring her back here at the end of the school day, so I can make sure Jack and Solomon collect her.' It seemed my day was planned out.

Everyone collected their bags and walked off for their lessons.

I followed Emily out of the room, and we headed for our first class, history. 'Of course, the history is all about Pontus Island and the rest of the Caribbean,' she said, 'it won't be about Kings and Queens of England or the Industrial Revolution - not the interesting stuff we're used to.'

Emily had moved to Pontus from London a few months earlier and was very quick to tell me about her family life.

'My father works in the British Consulate here. He's got a very important job. We lived in a big house in London before we moved to Pontus and now, we've got an enormous house here in St. Stephens.'

I was pleased she didn't ask me any questions about my background as I didn't want to reveal that I'd lived on the Bamford Estate in East London. I didn't feel I wanted to share any of my previous life with her, but despite being a bit snooty, Emily seemed friendly enough and looked after me during the day.

When I joined Jack and Solomon on the bus home, I had lots to talk about. 'I think the local children are very friendly, and my lessons were good too. I loved hearing about the history of Pontus and the story we had today was about a pirate ship that came here from Spain in 1700. It must have been very different here then, and even our teacher said that the actor Johnny Depp, was probably not at all like the real pirates.'

'Yeah, it's strange though, isn't it,' said Jack, 'when I arrived here from Australia, I expected the whole island to be like the Pirates of the Caribbean film! But I'm quite happy it's not like that, as I'd rather swim, snorkel and dive than have to be a swash-buckling hero. Their food didn't sound too tasty back then, either.'

'Always thinking of your stomach, Jack!' said Sol. 'Come on, let's get Lucy back and safely delivered to the Dive Centre. She can work for Dan while we go for a swim.'

From then on, my school days whizzed past, as I learnt more about where I'd come to live, as well as all the usual stuff like maths and science. The local pupils all spoke good English, so there was no problem with me understanding everyone and most of the children wanted to chat to me in order to practise their English.'

I sent texts back to Eve in London. 'I've settled into my new school,' I wrote. 'There are no girls being nasty to me and my uniform is very smart.' I also sent one a few days later ... 'I'm getting fed up with Emily telling me how posh her life is but I'm feeling more comfortable being friends with the local girls.' Eve replied that she was happy I was settling in and had new friends, but she had no news of real interest to tell me, and I realised I wasn't telling her half of what was happening to me, because there was so much to tell, and I couldn't text it all quickly enough. I kept my texts short and it wasn't long before I realised, I'd not sent her a text for some weeks. My past life in London soon seemed a distant memory as I accepted my new life and the challenges it was bringing. To be honest I wasn't missing Eve or my old life back in London at all.

CHAPTER FIFTEEN

Sea Creatures

My fears about my new life were diminishing. After school every day I would rush home to change, then eagerly head for the Dive Centre to start working with Dan and Rene.

Dan had told me about his other new member of staff, Bradley on my first day of working at the Dive Centre.

'You'll meet him soon,' he said. 'He's been quite helpful today. He dived with me this morning and acted like a sheep dog ... staying behind the students in the water to make sure they didn't get lost. He seems a reasonable sort of chap. His family work in St. Stephens so he goes back in the afternoons to help them. He starts early in the morning here though, checking out the equipment before the students arrive. I think he'll be quite useful.'

Certainly, Dan needed help and I'd been pleased that Bradley was working well, but I wasn't likely to meet him very often, as he was always gone by the time I arrived back from school.

I soon settled into working at the Dive Centre and Dan seemed pleased with my work. 'You've done well too, Lucy since you started. You've worked really hard,' he said. 'Divers are finding their kit easily now that you've sorted it out, and I'm selling more clothing and fish guidebooks, too.'

For me it was like playing shops, as I'd done when I was younger, so I was starting to enjoy myself.

However, when Dan began to teach me to swim, I realised how stupid I must seem for being so scared. He was always calm and patient and allowed me to take my time getting used to the water, but I still found it difficult and would panic at the slightest difficulty.

'You've done well with Jack and Sol, it's helped you to get used to the feel of the water,' he said, 'but now I'm going to get you to swim properly.'

He constantly encouraged me, forever smiling and trying to keep me focussed.

'That's it, now dip your head underneath.'

I forced myself to get my shoulders level with the surface and shut my eyes tight. It was so hard for me to put my head completely below the water. I struggled and held my nose as I eventually went down.

I was total rubbish. When the water got anywhere near my eyes, I squealed, stood up and started coughing and spluttering.

'No,' said Dan, 'keep your eyes open underwater. Simply let your eyes get used to the water.'

It sounded so simple, but when I tried to dip my head under the water I couldn't stop myself from shutting my eyes and that was so stupid, as I then couldn't see what I was doing or where I was going and I ended up struggling to stand up on the bottom of the pool.

I made slow progress in the first couple of days, but gradually managed to doggy-paddle around, trying to keep my chin well above the water. I stayed within my depth but still disliked getting water on my face and in my eyes.

Yet Dan even had a cure for this problem. He gave me a diving mask. I loved it as it kept the water away from my eyes.

Although my progress was slow, I was determined not to be beaten. Dan was incredibly kind, and I didn't want to let him down. I'd also promised Mum I'd learn to swim and wanted to please her with my efforts ... and there was also that inner voice, the voice which kept on nagging me.

It was a soft, gentle voice, repeating the words 'you'll be okay, be brave.' I kept hearing the inner voice encouraging me and eventually I did find myself swimming properly, but it took me another week of swimming practice before I could do a full length of the small pool and it certainly hadn't been easy.

Every day, when I finished my swimming lessons, I'd join Jack and Sol back at the beach. By now I had my own mask and snorkel and I joined the boys for the remainder of the afternoon practising my ability to snorkel.

'It's good that Dan insists you wear a buoyancy vest,' said Sol, 'it'll help you float.'

It certainly helped to give me a further boost of confidence as I knew I couldn't sink below the waves and drown and by now I'd also become more realistic about sea monsters.

Snorkelling kept me on the surface, in water that was lit by the sunshine. There certainly weren't any sea monsters in this top part of the water. The sunlight was chasing them away.

By looking down through the mask and breathing through the snorkel tube I could lie for ages watching the sea life which lived below the surface, on the strip of coral reef positioned just off the beach.

I loved searching for my favourite types of sea creatures and was fascinated by how many different types of fish were swimming nearby with small fish constantly surrounding me and darting in different directions.

Floating alongside me, Sol pointed at a large shoal of yellow snappers and I saw several elongated cornet fish hiding in the shoal. These strange fish were changing their normal pale grey colour to yellow to camouflage themselves amongst the yellow bodies of the snappers. They were swimming with their heads hanging downwards searching for food. I'd been reading about these fish in Dan's guidebook and it was incredible to see them in real life.

There were beautiful purple pipe sponges, hard dome corals and several large fan corals.

Jack pointed out a giant spider crab, with spines on its shell, scuttling along the sand, rushing to hide under the reef on the sandy seabed. I imagined it was hiding from predators and also waiting for any small fish to swim by, close enough for the crab to catch and eat them.

But I also got upset at the sight of so much rubbish caught up in the reef ... plastic bottles, straws, bags, sandwich wrappers and loads more were caught up in the coral crevices and it all reminded me of the day we rescued the turtle and how much the turtle had been suffering.

Both Jack and Sol tried to dive down to the reef to collect some of the rubbish, but most of it was too deep for them to reach whilst snorkelling.

As we swam back to the shore, we chatted about what we'd seen.

'Next time we come diving,' Jack said to Sol, 'we'll do a clean-up on the reef.'

'It's awful,' I said. 'If only those people who sit on the beach would realise what's happening to all their rubbish. Those creatures shouldn't have to put up with all this!'

Since our turtle rescue, Jack and I had regularly collected beach rubbish when Sol packed the chairs away and most days, we would fill at least half a bag.

'It's less than it was,' said Sol, 'I think people are taking notice of Grandpa when he's been asking them to take their rubbish home. That's good.'

We took the bag to the shed behind Drifters.

'What's that?' yelled Jack. 'That stuff wasn't there yesterday.'

He was looking at what looked like a big pile of cardboard on the beach near the road.

'It must have been dumped today.' said Sol. Look it's broken boxes with plastic inside and there's a lot of rotten fruit amongst it all.'

'It's attracting flies too,' I said, 'it's smelly, and look, there's a load of plastic bags in there, too.'

'Terrible,' said Jack. 'Why can't people take it to the proper areas in St. Stephens? This isn't the place to dump it. Whoever eats this much fruit must be a fruit bat.'

We muttered and mumbled as we cleaned it all away, but all agreed we had to clean it up to stop the plastic going into the sea.

I'd made a promise to the turtle about protecting it. I wasn't ever going to forget my promise, but I was sensing it was going to be a very hard challenge for me to achieve.

CHAPTER SIXTEEN

What's Next?

'Lucy, you've done a fantastic job in the shop,' said Dan, 'and you've also learnt to swim, so it's time for me to keep my side of our bargain.'

I turned to look at him. What was he going to say?

He was smiling and was obviously excited. 'I think you're ready for the next challenge. Your swimming will improve quickly now you've done a length of the pool. Start by reading the dive instruction book, then you'll be ready to learn to scuba dive.'

Did he mean it? Was he going to let me dive? Did he think I was ready?

Dan obviously saw my hesitant reaction.

'No, it's okay,' he explained. 'You don't need to be an expert swimmer to be able to dive. When diving, it's your fins that do all the work, not your arms. In fact, it's easier to swim underwater in dive kit than it is to swim on the surface. Once you learn how to use the dive equipment underwater ... you'll get stronger too ... so all your swimming skills will improve quickly.'

'Wow!' It was incredible ... not simply that Dan was going to teach me to go underwater, but my immediate reaction had been excitement rather than being scared! Perhaps my fear of the water was finally calming down. It seemed I wasn't so worried about going underwater ... in fact, there was even a bit of me that couldn't wait to start.

I knew Joel would be pleased for me too, because of all he'd told me about sea creatures in the waters around Dolphin Bay. It wasn't only dolphins I had a chance of seeing; it was sharks, manta rays, turtles and hundreds of assorted fish and amazing tiny creatures like coral and sea slugs. Yes ... sea slugs! Joel had already explained how much he loved them.

'Them cute little sea slugs, they're so colourful - not like them slimy, ol' black slugs you get in gardens back in England.'

I couldn't wait to see them and perhaps I'd be able to find my friend the turtle and swim alongside it.

I'd realised the voice I'd heard encouraging me to learn to swim was coming from a deep part of my brain. When I thought about helping the turtles it was as if I could hear a voice, encouraging me to achieve my new skills. I'd learnt to swim and was now about to enter the underwater world. My mind buzzed with ideas of what I would see but it still tried to play tricks on me ... imagining being trapped beneath the surface ... unable to return to the warm sunshine and fresh air.

Could I cope with going into the dark, deep cold of the underwater world?

The night before my first scuba lesson in the pool, I lay awake for ages. My brain jumped backwards and forwards between excitement at discovering new underwater creatures, then pure fright as I imagined the darkness and unknown monsters hiding in the dark depths.

In the morning, the sun chased the monsters out of my brain as Dan explained how the scuba equipment worked. I found the wetsuit difficult to pull on past my feet and up my legs and the mouthpiece tasted horrible, but I managed to keep it in my mouth by clamping my teeth around the moulded rubber, so I could breathe quite easily.

74

I also did NOT want to lose my mask whilst underwater, so I made sure the strap was adjusted properly around my head. The air tank was incredibly heavy on my back and it was difficult to walk in the fins.

'You're looking good to go,' said Dan as he checked the air hoses were attached to the tank properly and that I could breathe through the mouthpiece.

'Okay, Lucy?' he asked, as we both got ready to enter the pool.

'It's a bit scary.'

My worries had turned to words, but perhaps sharing my nervousness out loud would help?

'It's quite normal to be scared,' said Dan, 'you're entering an alien world. We don't have gills, so we can't get our oxygen from the water like fish do, so we must take all this life support system down with us. It all feels very strange though, doesn't it?'

I nodded my head like a toy dog ... so, being scared was normal ... that was really good to hear.

'Are you sure about this Dan?' I asked. 'I'm not a very strong swimmer yet.'

'That's not a problem,' said Dan, 'you don't need to be a strong swimmer. Diving's a completely different way of moving around in the water compared to being on the surface. You'll see in a minute, it's all about being weightless and moving around whilst the water surrounds you. You're not trying to swim just on the surface ... you're going under the water and taking your breathing apparatus with you, so you can stay there for about an hour.'

I nodded again but I was still frowning.

'It's okay, you've learnt all the safety stuff about diving, and I'll be looking after you. Don't worry, Lucy, you'll probably just feel like a fish out of water, to begin with.'

'I've never seen a fish in a wetsuit!' I giggled.

Our laughter broke the tension of my worries, and I made a conscious decision to stop worrying and enjoy the experience.

Sol and Jack turned up to watch my first dive in the pool.

'I think you need us in there too, Dan,' said Jack. 'We can help show Lucy what to do.'

'Okay, get kitted up and join in - it'll be more fun for Lucy if she's got you two around her. Right Lucy, are you ready? Head up, hold your hand against your mouthpiece to stop it coming out and look straight ahead. Just do a big stride forward and drop into the deep end of the pool.'

I stood at the edge of the pool ... this was it! I lifted my right leg into the air and stretched it out in front of me. Suddenly, I was in mid-air and falling towards the water. I probably only took a few milliseconds to hit the water, but it felt like I was moving in slow motion. My stomach churned and I squeezed by eyes tightly shut. No, you're right Dan, this isn't natural. What the heck was I doing!

I hit the water like an explosion and the shock made me breathe in quickly through my mouthpiece.

I was sinking!

CHAPTER SEVENTEEN

Weightless

Going underwater for the first time was terrifying. I needed to add it to my list of scariest things I'd ever done!

Gradually, my downward speed slowed. I kicked my fins and popped back up to the surface.

Dan, Jack and Sol splashed in around me and I was taught to descend below the surface, in a controlled way.

As I sank into the deep end of the pool, I got the strangest of feelings. There was water all around me ... above ... below ... everywhere, but I couldn't seem to feel it. I was floating; turning; moving without effort. When I'd been swimming on the surface, I'd felt I was fighting my way through the water, but here, it was peaceful and calm. My body seemed to weigh nothing at all. The air tank no longer felt heavy and I could move around so easily. Is this what weightlessness is all about? It was so crazy, to be free of the force of gravity, which normally kept my feet on the ground. Underwater I could easily turn somersaults and even stand on my head.

Jack and Sol came alongside me and together we spun and turned in every direction.

Dan used hand signals to tell me to swim up and down the pool, close to the bottom. I only had to kick my fins slowly, with my arms by my sides and I was moving smoothly through the water. When I breathed out, I could see my air bubbles racing to the surface. I now realised what Dan had meant when he said that diving was totally different to swimming on the surface. This was so much easier. Instead of trying not to sink and keeping my face above water so I could breathe easily, I was happy to sink beneath the water and breathe through my mouthpiece.

Whenever I looked at Dan, he was smiling. His eyes looked bigger through his mask and he constantly encouraged me, but I knew the skills training was still to come and I wasn't sure how I would cope with that.

I watched Sol demonstrate removing his mouthpiece and pushing the floating air hose away. Then he reached out to recover it, cleared it of water and used it to breathe air again. He made it look so easy.

He signalled for me to repeat his actions ... but as soon as I pushed my mouthpiece and air hose away from me ... I felt I needed to breath, and I struggled to keep my mouth tightly shut. My lungs began to burn. I needed air, but I couldn't reach my air supply. As I moved towards the mouthpiece, it floated further away from me ... my arm seemed to have shrunk ... I couldn't reach it.

Sol quickly came alongside and showed me how to pull on the hose to bring it closer. Phew! Mouthpiece back in ... air supply restored ... lungs receiving air ... that's better!

I'd been really scared ... why hadn't I thought of pulling on the part of the hose that was closest to me? How stupid was that!

Dan made me practise losing my mouthpiece again and again until I became more confident. I surprised myself by getting better quite quickly ... perhaps it was because I never wanted to feel pain in my lungs ever again.

My first dive lasted about thirty minutes with Jack and Sol demonstrating the underwater skills I needed. The training was all about coping with emergencies underwater ... losing your air or getting equipment trapped whilst underwater. I got a bit tangled up when I had to remove, then replace, my buoyancy jacket and tank, but I mostly completed all the skills without too many problems.

When we'd finished my training, we emerged from the pool into the bright sunshine, soon drying off and chatting about my progress.

'You've done really well today, Lucy,' said Dan. 'Now you know how to handle the equipment, it'll be useful at weekends if you put the students' equipment away when we come back from a dive,' he said.

Sol and Jack taught me how to clear up, and I hosed the equipment I'd used with fresh water, pretending I'd been in the sea and was washing the salt off. Jack and Sol did the same, but somehow got themselves into a hose-pipe water fight, getting each other very wet.

Dan raised his eyebrows and shook his head, muttering 'Boys!'

I watched. I was thinking ahead. Perhaps it wouldn't be too long before I could dive in the sea properly or go out and help Dan's students on the boat.

When we'd finished with the dive equipment, Jack and Sol told me that they'd found yet another pile of fruit boxes and plastic rubbish by the beach road.

'Yeah,' said Jack, 'we didn't tell you before as you were busy with your diving lessons, but our fruit bat-rubbish-dumper is still around. That's been three times now, same stuff, same place. I think we need to keep an eye out and see if we can catch whoever's doing it.'

Mum was waiting to hear of my progress and I soon forgot about the litter as I explained what I'd been doing.

'I can swim underwater,' I gasped. 'I was able to swim around just like a fish or dolphin. It's so much easier than swimming on the surface. My mask fitted well, so there was no water getting in my eyes. It was like being in a mystical world.'

Mum was smiling.

'It's amazing, Mum, to be under the water and yet still be able to breathe air into my mouth. I loved it! Dan says the astronauts who travelled to the moon had to train as scuba divers first. They had to practice being weightless, the same as I did underwater today.

'You're doing well, Lucy,' she said, 'and I'm really proud of you.'

A few days later, Dan said I'd completed my pool training, and Jack and Sol begged Dan to let them come and join me on my first ever dive in the sea.

As we were collecting our gear Jack updated me on what they'd been doing. 'We've tried to watch out for the litter being dropped, but it's always done too early in the morning for us to see who's done it, but today Sol noticed the mess has been dumped at the far end of the Dive Centre, out of sight around the back.'

'I noticed it when I was helping Dan with the tanks,' said Sol. 'I'm sure it's the same stuff.'

'We'll get your first dive done, then later maybe we'll have time to sit and talk to Joel,' said Jack, 'he might have some ideas.'

We took our equipment and set off down the beach. Dan's plan was to take the boat out a few hundred metres, drop the anchor into a sandy patch of seabed, then dive down to the local reef below.

We walked along the wooden jetty which led from the edge of the beach over the deeper seawater to where Dan's dive boat was moored up.

Would I see beautiful sea creatures or scary monsters? I remembered the diver who weeks ago had told the story of the moray eel with the big teeth jumping out at him from a crack in the coral. Hopefully, I wouldn't meet up with a moray eel or be attacked by any other weird underwater monster which might be lurking.

I told myself not to panic. I had to stay calm!

80

CHAPTER EIGHTEEN

Alien World

We started the engine and made our way out to the reef. Dan secured the anchor, kitted up and stepped off the back of the boat. His splash made a loud noise and he disappeared below the water. Within seconds, his head bobbed up above the surface as he waited for us to join him.

Jack put his mouthpiece in and protected it with the palm of his hand to stop it being dislodged as he splashed into the water.

I made sure my air tank was switched on and transferred some air into my dive jacket. I clamped my teeth around my mouthpiece ... then did what I'd practised in the pool ... I stepped forward and took a giant stride into the air, entering the water feet first.

My splash felt enormous and water swirled around the outside of my mask. I sank at least three metres down below the surface before the air in my dive jacket stopped me from sinking any further. I looked up, kicked my fins and surfaced to feel the sun shining on my face.

As Sol joined us, Dan gave the diver's okay sign. 'Ready?'

We all returned the okay sign and nodded. Pulling on my dump valve I released air from my buoyancy jacket, and I slowly sank beneath the waves.

Entering the underwater ocean world was different to diving in the pool as I could see way into the distance. As the sunlight shone through the water from the surface, sharp, straight rays of light dispersed and quickly changed to moving flashes in the water as they disappeared beneath us. I clamped my mouth securely around my air supply. My breathing rate felt too fast. If I didn't slow my breathing, I'd use up my air supply up too quickly.

Dan signalled for me to be calm. I took a big deep breath, exhaling slowly. That was better. I watched as bubbles noisily exited through my breathing equipment, passing my mask and heading for the surface.

We all kept together as we descended. The boys buddied up and Dan stayed close to me.

A shoal of small black and white striped fish dashed around my mask. They were beautiful, but they seemed very close to my face. Did these fish bite?

Were my ears safe, or were they going to take bites out of me as they swam around my head?

We dropped to fifteen metres below the surface. I squirted a tiny amount of air into my jacket. I'd stopped sinking and levelled off. I swam slowly, looking at different fish as they swam around the reef. The bigger fish were taking no notice of us, at all ... just swimming around, going about their business, looking for food and avoiding predators.

Some bright red, soft coral gently swayed in the breeze-like current in the water, and I was surrounded by fish of different varieties, sizes, shapes and colours darting in and out of the crevices of the hard coral. I couldn't decide where to look first. I saw Dan watching me. He must have known how excited I felt, realising I'd never experienced anything like this before in my life, but there was a shadow over my thoughts. I enjoyed the diving and watching the sea creatures, but I couldn't bear the amount of rubbish I saw as I swam over the reef.

Dan needed me to prove I could do the technical skills he'd taught me in the pool, but this time, doing them in the open water of the sea. I breathed in deeply then took my mouthpiece out. The hose with my air supply was floating away from me. This was so dangerous. At fifteen metres below the surface, I had to get this right. If I couldn't get my air supply back in my mouth this time, then I'd gulp mouthfuls of salty water and could drown. I pulled on the hose and gulped in the air. Phew! Mission accomplished.

Jack and Sol watched, and both gave me the thumb and finger 'okay' sign.

Then the task I dreaded even more. I had to take my mask off completely, wait for a minute, then put it back on and remove the seawater from inside.

Although I completed the task to show Dan I could do it, not wearing a mask over my eyes and nose made me suddenly breathe quicker. I was relying on my mask to keep the water out of my eyes and nose. I felt scared when I was without it. I floundered around holding my nose to stop any water going in and choking me. I screwed my eyes up in panic. When I opened them the salt water stung and everything seemed blurry. I was desperate to get the mask back on my face and open my eyes properly.

I made a conscious decision to never, ever lose my mask.

When I'd completed all the skills, we returned to the surface and climbed the ladder back onto the dive boat. Dan ticked boxes on the list of practical diving skills I had to achieve. 'That's it, Lucy, you've done everything. All that's left is the written exam, then you can be a qualified Open Water Diver.'

Brilliant, I was almost there ... I'd soon be able to help the sea creatures!

All I had to do now was pass the exam! I'd never had to pass an exam before. My stomach did double, triple and quadruple somersaults ... this was a crazy feeling. I hadn't thought it possible to be this nervous.

CHAPTER NINETEEN

Testing Time

Running out of the school gates, I was breathing fast by the time I'd reached my bus stop. Great, I'd managed to beat Jack and Solomon. It was a daily competition which I normally lost. I checked my watch. Five minutes, then the bus to Jude's Bay would arrive.

I waved to Emily as her posh car passed the bus stop. At the end of every school day, Emily would get picked up at the school and be driven away to disappear behind the high-security gates of the Embassy building, returning to her parents and baby brother.

Our lives were very different, so in class we didn't chatter much about what happened to us outside of school. I'd soon decided Emily wasn't going to be a close friend and I certainly hadn't told Emily everything about my life because when I'd told her I was learning to swim she hadn't been at all interested.

'Well, everyone can swim, that's not special news,' she'd snapped. 'Our home has its own private pool and I swim there most afternoons. I wouldn't dream of swimming in the sea.'

She was being snooty and snobbish, so I didn't argue or try to share my understanding of the ocean with her. She had already made her mind up that the ocean didn't suit her posh lifestyle and she'd probably never discover how spectacular the animals were.

I certainly didn't share how happy I was going to the Dive Centre every afternoon. I didn't share how I felt so free, or how my life had changed in the weeks since I'd been working with Dan. Afraid that Emily would dismiss my efforts as unimportant, I kept my excitement to myself until reaching the bus stop where my life out of school began.

I'd finished all my diver training in the pool and the sea, so this afternoon I was taking my diver's exam. Hopefully, if I got the answers right, I'd become a qualified diver.

Jack and Solomon caught up with me at the bus stop. When our bus got to Jude's Bay, we jumped off to go our separate ways.

'Good luck with the exam,' said Sol, quietly.

Jack gave me a high five. 'You'll be fine,' he said. 'See you later.'

I rushed home to change before heading to the Dive Centre, then sat alone under a large sun umbrella at a wooden table near the pool. I started the exam paper.

The first question looked easy. Was it a trick or had I really understood and learnt what I needed to know? Gradually I worked my way through the questions. I soon realised the easy questions were at the beginning and they got harder. I was unsure of a few of the answers near the end but decided to half-guess them. There! Finished! There was nothing more I could do.

I went into the Dive Centre to find Dan and he exchanged my exam paper for a can of fizzy drink.

'Okay, I'll mark it and tell you how you got on when we meet up at Drifters later.'

I wandered back home, not quite sure what to do with myself. I was desperate to get my scuba diver's certificate. I'd loved my first dive in the ocean and wanted to do much, much more. I'd struggled on a few questions, but I hoped I'd done enough to pass? I wasn't convinced though.

We ate our meal quietly.

'Well, you've done your best,' said Mum, 'and we'll soon find out how you got on.'

I pushed the food around my plate. I couldn't eat. I simply wasn't hungry.

When we walked to Drifters, we found Joel sitting with Jack and his parents, Pete and Mel. Mum sat one side of me, her arm around my shoulder, and when Sol arrived, he squeezed in by my other side. It was like Mum and my friends were all supporting me, almost holding me up. I was desperate to pass so I could go diving with Jack and Solomon.

When Dan arrived, he looked very serious. My stomach turned over and I felt sick. Did I really want to know the result? Could I take the disappointment?

'Well everyone,' said Dan, frowning. 'I think I'd better let you know ... despite all my best efforts, I'm afraid to tell you that Lucy has ...'

The silence allowed loud rhythmic beats to echo in my head. Bang, bang, bang ... was that my heartbeat? Could I hear the blood streaming through my arteries? Dan's words appeared to slow down. I must have failed ... he must be trying to break it to me gently.

Then suddenly he was smiling as he spoke. Dan's voice sounded a long way away. 'Lucy has ... passed her scuba exam. Well done, Lucy.'

Sound returned to normal as everybody cheered loudly. Mum hugged me tight, then everyone joined in the hug and I was trapped in a breath-squeezing moment, in the middle of all the people I loved the most.

I'd passed! I'd really passed!

I took a deep breath and tried to jump up and down, but everyone was still hugging me, laughing and cheering. Oh, what a feeling!

I couldn't believe it. I'd done it. I was a qualified diver.

Mum giggled as she looked at Dan. 'Do I get to see my daughter sometimes, now?' she asked.

I heard Dan laugh gently. 'Once she'd beaten her fear of swimming, she was able to concentrate quickly on the diving skills. I know, it's not been easy for her,' I heard him say, 'but I'm so pleased with her progress, and now she'll be even more useful around the Dive Centre.'

Joel interrupted my earwigging and spoke quietly.

'So, young Lucy,' he said, 'you've successfully dealt with your first challenge ... you can swim and dive now, so you've started on your journey. Remember, when you looked that turtle in the eye, you made a promise. You've gotta help those turtles and all those other sea creatures. There's a lot of work to be done. You're a clever young lady and you gotta learn to be brave, make decisions and take the lead. That way you'll be able to help your turtle friend.'

I nodded. 'Yes, Joel, I made a promise and I'm determined to keep it.'

Trouble was, I had no idea where to start?

CHAPTER TWENTY

Bradley

Dan had employed Bradley to drive the boat out to the dive sites, then help the students get into their dive kit and into the water, but after the first few weeks since he'd employed him, Dan was starting to lose his patience with Brad's laziness. Dan had mumbled and moaned one day that Brad had developed a very poor work attitude.

'I take the lead during the dive, and he's supposed to be at the back checking the students are okay, but I've looked back a few times and he's nowhere to be seen. He's always back on the boat first but doesn't help the students out of the water. Back here at the Dive Centre he's supposed to refill all the air tanks and wash the dive kit, but he usually disappears before he does any of the clearing up work.'

I'd never heard Dan quite so cross.

'He's always doing the least he possibly can to help either the students or me,' said Dan. 'It seems he wants to take the money from the students without actually earning it.'

Bradley's laziness meant I gained the extra job of hosing down the hired kit the students had used in the mornings and hanging it up to dry. Dan also decided to employ Solomon to refill the air tanks in the afternoons. Solomon was so reliable, and he enjoyed making a few extra dollars helping Dan before it was time for him to pack away his Grandpa's sunbeds.

Once I had my diver's qualification, Dan decided to let me dive with him at weekends, so I could gain experience.

It was when I worked on the dive boat for my first Saturday morning, that I eventually met Bradley, face to face. It was strange. As soon as I met him, I felt uncomfortable. Bradley seemed different to everyone else I'd met on the Island. He wouldn't look me straight in the eye when he spoke to me, he didn't seem to smile much and was never friendly. In fact, he hardly said anything to me at all, but when he did speak, his mouth sneered at me. He was someone I felt I couldn't trust. I was always as polite as I could be to him, but I tried to keep away from him as much as possible.

On the second Saturday morning, when we were both out on the dive boat, Bradley came over as I put on my scuba gear.

'Your mask is too loose,' he said, so he tightened it, by pulling the side straps which adjusted how it fitted on my face. I accepted what he said without question, as he was a far more experienced diver than I was ... but I regretted that decision later.

I was twenty metres down and diving at the front of the students with Dan when I felt the mask starting to hurt my face. The pressure of the water was pushing on the mask. I realised there was red liquid inside my mask, and I could hardly see through it. I cleared the mask through seawater and then emptied it just as I had done in my training, but within minutes the mask was full of red liquid again. My head had started to really hurt, my eyes were aching, and I began to feel dizzy. This was now starting to get dangerous. Twenty metres underwater was not a good time to be feeling that my world was spinning around.

Dan realised something was wrong and he signalled for all the student divers to go up whilst he helped me to the surface. As we popped up out of the water, he got me to remove the mask.

I was horrified ... the mask was full of blood. 'Don't panic, Lucy,' said Dan. 'You've had a nose bleed and your face looks bruised too. Looks like your mask was too tight. You'll have a headache for a while, but you'll be okay.'

I felt relieved to be back safely on the boat. The nosebleed was stopping at last and as I cleaned the blood from my face, I realised just how dangerous my situation had been. I was so angry and knew exactly why my mask had been too tight ... Bradley! He'd done it on purpose. When he climbed back on board, I glared at him and he laughed in my face.

'Not so clever now are you, Miss Clever Clogs,' he said quietly, so only I could hear him. Then he called across to Dan, and I couldn't believe what he was saying.

'I told you she was useless,' he was telling Dan. 'She's a danger underwater to herself and everyone else. We stopped the dive today because her. She can't even wear her mask properly without causing herself a problem.'

Dan looked back towards me and frowned. Surely, he didn't believe all that rubbish. Or maybe Brad was right ... should I have noticed how tight my mask was? Should I have adjusted it underwater? Oh, I disliked Brad so much now. Why was he so horrible to me? This was worse than the bullying I'd had in my London school. I'd disliked it then, but in London it was only words and glaring. This event had been physical. I'd been hurt and put in a hazardous situation.

Dan must have now thought I was an idiot and even perhaps damaging his business as he had to stop the dive, but I couldn't admit to Dan that I'd been hood-winked by Bradley. I felt such a fool, but I'd never trust Bradley ever again. Luckily, Dan was too busy to talk about it again that day, so I hoped it would all be forgotten.

CHAPTER TWENTY-ONE

The Fruit Bat Dumper

Jack and Sol came to sit either side of Joel and me.

'What's up boys?' Joel asked.

'We've got a mystery to solve Grandpa, and we need your help,' said Sol.

We explained the fruit bat dumper situation and Joel sat thoughtfully scratching at his chin full of stubble.

'Umm,' he said, 'that's a strange one, but my money's on a fruit stall in St. Stephens market. That market's open most days.'

'But doesn't the market have bins? Why isn't this person putting their rubbish in the bins there?' I asked.

'Ah, they've got a strange system at that market,' said Joel. 'The stallholders ... they pays for their space to sell their goods, but the price to use the rubbish bins is extra. Maybe this dumper person just don't wanna spend the extra money, or they're just too darn lazy to carry it over to the rubbish site.'

'I reckon Sol and I need to go after school and search for who it could be,' said Jack. 'We'll go tomorrow and see what we can find out. Lucy, you need to get back here as usual to work at the Dive Centre, and I'll help Sol refill the tanks later.

I travelled home on the bus by myself the next day, hoping the boys would find out something which would identify our mystery litter dumper. As I stepped into the

Dive Centre, I saw Bradley. He'd usually gone by the time I got there so our paths had rarely crossed.

'Hi,' I said, quietly.

He looked straight at me and wagged his finger. 'You,' he said, 'you gonna be taking my job next.'

I had no idea what he was talking about, but he scared me because he looked so angry. What had I done?

'Dan'll end up giving you my Saturday job, won't he? You've told him you don't like me, and he'll listen to your opinion, rather than mine.'

'I've said nothing to Dan,' I said, 'you've no right to accuse me of anything.'

'We'll, it'll be me with no work at weekends and not getting paid. You're a bundle of trouble you are.' He stormed past me and pushed my shoulder so hard I nearly fell over. He slammed the door of the Dive Centre so hard I thought the glass would break.

I felt tears coming into my eyes. How could he be so nasty to me? I went through to the equipment room and spoke to Dan.

'What's the matter with Bradley?' I asked. 'He seems angry with me.'

'Umm, he seems to be angry with everyone at the moment. I've noticed he's got a terrible temper too. I'm not sure he and I are going to get along much longer. He's incredibly lazy. He's only here this afternoon because I insisted he finished off the jobs he's supposed to do. I'm not impressed with him at all.'

An hour later, Sol and Jack trooped in. Both were smiling. We sat at a patio table at the back of the Dive Centre.

'Got him,' said Jack, smiling

'Who?' I asked.

'Our fruit bat dumper, of course. We're almost sure we know who it is.'

'Oh yes, of course. What happened?' I asked. I was annoyed that Bradley's attitude had affected my memory of the important detective task that Sol and Jack had been doing.

'We went over to the market after school and walked around,' said Sol 'We found three fruit stalls and we looked carefully at the boxes they all used but only one of them had boxes printed with the name we get on the dumped rubbish.'

'The market started to close,' said Jack, 'and everyone was packing away so we stayed and watched this one stall ... and guess who came driving up?'

'Who? Who was it?' I was becoming impatient. 'Tell me.'

'Bradley!' said Jack.

'What, the Bradley who works for Dan, here? He was really horrible to me this afternoon and left in a real temper.'

'That's him ... he seemed in a right mood when he got to the market too,' said Jack. 'He was shouting at people about something. I think they were his Dad and brother. There was a big family argument. Then he picked up the rubbish and started throwing it into his truck. It's him. Bradley is the fruit bat dumper.'

'What's all this about?' said Dan as he came out on the patio.

Sol and Jack explained the whole story of the dumped litter, and what they had found out at St. Stephens market.

'I think we need to catch him dumping it here, before we accuse him of all this,' said Dan. 'Look, it's Saturday tomorrow and he's due in about seven o'clock. I'll get up early. If he dumps the stuff here again, I'll catch him, and he won't get off lightly either.'

Next morning, Sol and Jack were proved right. Dan explained everything to us. 'Bradley turned up and started to empty his truck right beside the Dive Centre,' said Dan, 'I was there to see it all. I told him I was fed up with his attitude to work and now I'd caught him littering as well. I made him put it all back into his truck and ordered him to drive it away to a proper disposal area. I also said he wasn't to come back ... he'd lost his job. I don't need someone like him working for me.'

I was so relieved Brad wasn't returning to the Dive Centre, I almost cheered.

I never wanted to see him again.

The following day was a quiet Sunday, with no divers booked in so I left Dan working in the equipment room and walked back into the reception area to finish tidying books and tee-shirts.

I found Bradley in the Dive shop with his hand in the till.

I'd caught him red-handed and we stared at each other. 'What are you doing?' I asked, in a cracking voice. I suddenly felt very scared as he glared across at me.

'Nothing for you to worry your silly little head about,' sneered Brad.

'But you don't have anything to do with the money in here. Dan's sacked you. You shouldn't even be here. You're stealing,' I accused him.

He grabbed most of the dollars out of the till and pushed them into his pocket. Within seconds he had hurdled across the counter and pushed me up against the wall with his hands around my neck.

It all happened so quickly that I didn't have time to draw a breath. I couldn't call out to Dan for help.

'You keep quiet, ok? You ain't seen nothing, right? You tell anyone what you seen, you gonna be a dead girl. Got it?'

I would've been shaking but he was pushing me so hard against the wall, I could hardly move. His hand was so tight over my mouth, I couldn't make any noise. I just nodded slightly, and my wide eyes tried to give him the message that I understood.

At that moment Rene came through the adjoining door from The Beach Shack.

She didn't seem to take in what she was seeing straight away. Then she realised what was happening and screamed very loudly.

Brad threw me down onto the floor and ran out of the front door.

Dan came rushing through from the equipment room. When he heard what had happened, he was angry but calmed down enough to check that I was alright.

'I'm so sorry Lucy, are you sure you're ok? Heck, your Mum's gonna kill me for this,' he looked so worried. 'She thinks I'm looking after you and here am I with a thief and hooligan going around threatening you.'

'It's ok?' I said, 'I'm fine, really I am … just a bit shaken up, but I'm really pleased he's gone.'

'I'm sure he won't come back here, so don't worry. I'll have the police onto him for hurting you and for stealing too.' Dan was still looking worried.

'I'm not hurt at all,' I said. 'Honest. I didn't even get a scratch. I just felt a bit scared that's all.'

Solomon walked in and looked around, 'What's all the fuss?' he asked. When he found out I was okay, he just smiled. 'He's really gone for good? Great! That means I've got a job every afternoon filling tanks. Isn't that right Dan?'

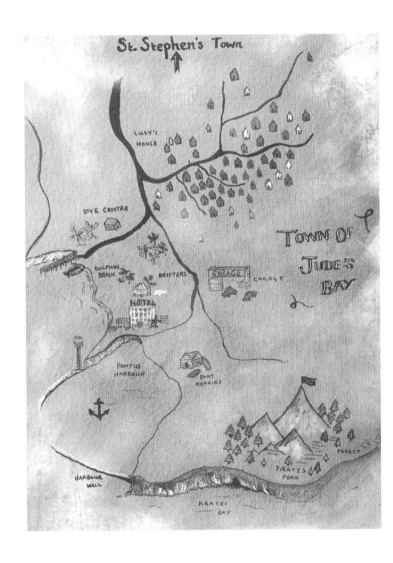

PART 2

CHAPTER TWENTY-TWO

Saturday Morning - Three months later

I had my eyes closed, remembering a dive where I'd watched stingrays flying past me, when the rooster in the next-door garden started to crow. It roused me from my dream-like mood. I stretched and turned over. My life on Pontus had settled into a regular routine - home, school, Dive Centre and Drifters and since becoming qualified, I'd regularly dived with Sol and Jack after school and sometimes Dan came with us too.

'I need to check you're still being careful and using your equipment correctly,' said Dan, 'and not getting slapdash about looking after yourselves.'

Dan had taught Sol and Jack to dive about six months before me, so we were all fairly new to our underwater adventures. Every time we dived, we saw incredible sea creatures.

In the evenings, we'd sit with Joel and flick through Dan's fish guidebooks, looking for information on the new creatures we'd seen that afternoon. Joel would tell us wonderful stories about the lives of these animals and how they interacted with each other.

'Some of them bigger ones, they're the predators, they goes chasing and eating the littler fish. Then you got the cute little ones, they're always prey for something ... they get chased and eaten if they don't get into a crack in the coral and hide quickly.'

'That's just what happens when we're diving, Joel,' I said. 'The little fish always swim away from us and hide in the coral. They must think we're predators and want to eat them.'

'That's it, Lucy. To them little fish, you probably look like a big black grouper or barracuda.'

I held on to everything Joel said when he was talking about sea creatures. I was becoming addicted to diving and determined to learn as much as I could about the underwater world.

There was still some litter being left on the beach, but Joel's requests to his customers to take their litter home and our occasional litter clean-ups had certainly helped to reduce it all. The fruit bat dumping had, of course, stopped as soon as Bradley had been arrested, and the last we heard about him was he'd been sent to jail for three months for illegal littering, stealing from Dan and assaulting me.

The amount of litter we saw underwater still worried me though. The three of us picked up everything we could find, whenever we dived. We each had special cloth bags that Mum had made for us and we never came up without having something inside them. I made sure I collected all the plastic bags I could find, as it always reminded me of my turtle friend. If only people could understand and see what we could see underwater. As I lie snoozing in bed, I made a decision. I was going to do more to stop rubbish being dumped in the ocean ... I wanted to help people to understand the ocean world ... get them to love it, like I did.

I looked at the clock. Six a.m. already. I jumped out of bed. There was no school on Saturday, but I was eager to start the day.

As I pulled back my curtains, the bright light made me blink. The trees surrounding our home were waving their branches gently in the breeze. I watched as sunlight danced through the trees and passed through my window creating shifting patterns on my wall.

I took a long look at my bedroom. Although not large, my room was very colourful. Mum had decided Pontus was an island full of colour and she wanted to show those colours around our home. She'd bought lots of different material from the market and I'd chosen a vivid green and orange pattern for my curtains and bed cover.

Zebbie always had a special place near my pillow, so Mum made him a tiny sleeping bag from the same material. I'd laughed when I first saw it and told her how Zebbie would love sleeping in it.

'Well,' she'd said, 'I reckoned a little bit of colour in that zebra's life wouldn't go amiss. His life's been very black and white ... up 'til now.'

I smiled at the memory. This had been a sign of Mum returning to her normal self. She'd become far less stressed now than when we'd been in London and had relaxed into her new job and our surroundings. She could be herself again, showing her daft sense of humour.

I dressed quickly, wondering what would happen to me today. Whatever it was, it was bound to include the pool, or the sea, so ... swimsuit, shorts, tee shirt, sandals ... yep, ready to go.

I took Mum a cup of tea. She didn't need to get up for at least an hour, but she smiled as soon as she opened her eyes.

'Oh, thank you Lucy. A strong cup of tea will start my day really well.' She was only just awake, yet already smiling broadly.

'It's great to see you happy again, Mum,' I said, 'and you always seem happiest on the days you're doing the language workshops.' I knew she'd be working all day at the Community Library. A special 'Improve Your English' day had been organised and she was running workshops for the locals who had signed up to take part.

'You're right, I do enjoy these days. The locals are so keen. I love helping them. You have a good day too and I'll see you later. Be careful.'

'Yeah, of course,' I said, '… always am.'

I had a quick drink of water and closed the door quietly as I left. As I crossed the road and walked towards the Dive Centre, I remembered I still hadn't told Mum about Emily's invitation. Emily had taken me aside at school.

'My mum works as a fashion model,' she'd said, 'she's actually very famous. I think I'd like to do that when I get a job. It means you travel all over the world to do the big fashion shows. It's a very glamorous life. I know I'd enjoy it.'

'Does that mean your Mum is away from home a lot?' I asked. I was trying to be polite and at least sound interested.

'Oh, yes. She's often away, but we have a nanny, Jilly, who looks after George and me while she's away and she always brings presents for us when she gets back home. Jilly said this morning that whilst Mum's away this time, I could invite a friend to tea after school next week. I thought you might want to come and see where I live? If you've learnt to swim now you could swim in our big pool.'

What on earth could I say! I didn't want to be rude, but I wasn't interested at all in going to tea, or swimming in her pool, and anyway, I worked at the Dive Centre every day after school. I'd much rather be having fun there, then swimming with Jack and Solomon afterwards, looking at lots of sea creatures. I tried to explain politely that I couldn't go.

'What do you mean? You can't come because you have to work? That sounds ridiculous! It can't be much fun for you being so poor that you have to work. But I suppose if you can't come ... I'll just find someone else who can.'

Emily strutted off before I could say anything else. Snooty little madam!

I didn't think Mum and I were poor. Our lives had changed since living in London and although Mum didn't earn a fortune, we had enough money for everything we needed and more importantly we had good friends and after school I had a great life. I decided Emily needed to understand the world a little more as she had no idea what a normal life, like mine, was like. As I walked through the door of the Dive Centre, I decided to forget Emily and her fancy talk. I had better things to think about. I decided I'd catch up with Joel when he was free and ask his advice. I needed to work out how to help people understand more about the sea ... and how we could stop people from littering the oceans?

CHAPTER TWENTY-THREE

The Beach Shack

I started work at six-thirty a.m., helping Dan restock the shelves of The Beach Shack ready for the day's trade in beach paraphernalia.

'We're surrounded by it, Dan,' I said.

'By what?'

'Plastic,' I said. 'Everything's plastic ... buckets, spades, swimming rings, armbands. The only thing you seem to sell, that isn't plastic, is the ice cream!'

'I hadn't thought of it that way,' said Dan. 'I've only stocked the shop with stuff the holidaymakers ask for. It's not occurred to me to think about plastic pollution.'

'We'll need to brainstorm. You need to make money from selling things that won't harm the sea animals.'

Dan looked so sad.

'I can't believe it's never occurred to me. I'm such an idiot for not noticing what I was doing. You kids will have to nag us adults, you know. What you're saying is important and it doesn't even occur to us we're causing damage to the environment.'

'It must be difficult to change things you've always done,' I said. 'Perhaps it's got to be us ... we're the next generation, aren't we? Maybe, we need to kick-start doing things differently. Don't worry, I can nag you a lot, if that helps.'

'Great, thanks, Lucy, I'll really look forward to that,' he said. He shook his head and grinned.

We'd nearly finished, and I was completing the task I always left to last... blowing up inflatable blue dolphin and green crocodile swimming toys and hanging them from the hooks on the ceiling. My least favourite job. Every time I blew air into them, my cheeks ached.

'Well, I hope these don't end up in the crevices of a coral reef,' I said.

'Okay, let's start now,' said Dan. 'Don't put them on display. We won't sell them anymore.'

'Great,' I said.

'If I make less profit from my business, I'll just have to pay you less,' said Dan.

'Hey, you don't pay me in money anyway,' I said, 'you pay me by letting me borrow snorkelling or dive equipment.'

Dan just grinned. 'Oh yeah, can't save money there then, can I?'

'We'll have to think hard about what you can sell. Ice cream. Beach clothing. You'll have to sell suncream in re-useable bottles and have a refill machine. Same with water. Perhaps the local traders who wander along the beach can make some wooden spades for the kids. That'll help their businesses too.'

'We can discuss it with everyone over dinner tonight if we all meet up in Drifters,' said Dan. 'Everyone can help us make decisions.'

'Good idea.'

I heard footsteps thumping up the steps and entering the shop.

'G'day. How ya doin,' came a loud shout. Jack had arrived.

'You and your daft Australian accent. Why can't you just say, 'Good morning' like everyone else,' I said.

'My Australian accent is not half as bad as your la-dee-da one from England. You sound like the Queen.'

'Well, that's perfect seeing as my middle name is Elizabeth, so I actually have the name of two Queens of England.'

'What are you burbling on about?' said Jack.

'Trust you to always turn up when I've nearly finished the work.' I answered.

Jack laughed. He could always get away with not helping as much as I did because Dan was his uncle.

'Yeah, yeah, yeah' he said, 'and you've loved every minute of being in here, fussing about and making it look all smart. Why am I having to listen to this nonsense from a dumb girl?' he said.

I glared and wrinkled up my nose. 'Dumb boy,' I muttered. I decided not to say anything else or it would only make Jack worse.

Dan started laughing. 'You two crack me up. Do you ever agree on anything?' he asked.

Jack smiled. 'Well, I suppose if it's anything to do with the sea or surfing,' he said.

'Or fish or any underwater sea creatures,' I suggested.

'Or snorkelling,' responded Jack.

'Or DIVING.' We managed to say this at exactly the same time, which made us look at each other and laugh even more.

'I know you were born on opposite sides of the world to different parents, but you act exactly like a brother and sister,' said Dan, as he joined in the laughter.

'Yuk! No way,' Jack pulled a face. 'No way am I related to a dumb girl.'

I threw him a scary glance and then decided to ignore him.

'Okay, you two,' Dan said. 'I know you both agree diving is wonderful and I think you're my best dive team, so I'll buy you breakfast.'

Dan looked around the shop. 'Rene will soon be here to open up the shop. Jack, just come over here and help Lucy for a bit, take the air out of these toys.'

'Haven't you just finished blowing them up?' queried Jack.

'Yep ... but Dan's decided to stop selling all the plastic stuff,' I said. 'If we pack it all up, he'll take it to the tip.'

'Just put it all back in the storeroom for now ... I'll sort it out later,' said Dan. 'I think we've done everything else. The shelves look a bit bare, but we'll soon sort that out. Thanks, Lucy. Let's go, before you two start arguing again.'

'Yeah, breakfast sounds good,' said Jack.

'Well, make the most of it,' said Dan. 'If I can't sell half my stock then I'll have less money next week. You'll have to buy me breakfast instead.'

'I'm sure we'll find alternative things to sell though, Dan,' I said. 'You'll probably be selling other stuff by next weekend and it'll all be so much better if it doesn't harm the sea creatures.'

CHAPTER TWENTY-FOUR

Breakfast at Drifters

'Mmm ... smells good,' said Jack, as we entered. The smell of freshly cooked bacon hung in the air.

Dan ordered drinks whilst our food was cooked.

'Your coffee smells disgusting, Dan,' said Jack. He screwed his nose up. 'I'm not having that.' He ordered an orange fizzy drink and took a blue plastic straw from the bar counter. We'd both been caught out before. The fizzy drinks were served in thin squidgy plastic cups and when we picked them up, the cups would start to collapse, spilling most of the fizzy drink over us. Jack was obviously protecting his knees by drinking with a straw.

'Need an itchy, witchy little baby straw do you?' I teased.

'Argh,' Jack groaned. 'Trust you to be sensible with a can of drink.'

'Yep, I'm not going to spill a thing!' I laughed, 'and the can is recyclable.'

'Seriously though, Jack, I think we need to stop using plastic straws and cups. Our experience with the turtle shows that plastics are dangerous near the ocean wildlife.'

Jack frowned. 'Yep, you're probably right,' then he started to laugh again. 'It hurts me to tell you that. I can't believe I've told a GIRL that she could be right! 'Grrr,' he growled, and shook his head. 'I can't believe I just said that.'

Jack's bap eventually arrived. 'Pass the red bottle, please,' he asked.

I watched him smother his roll with tomato sauce. 'Bet you spill ketchup down your tee shirt too,' I said, trying to get in the last word, but Jack was concentrating so hard on eating his breakfast, he'd stopped listening to me.

Dan shared his plans for the day. 'There're no dive students booked in, so I'm doing maintenance on the main dive boat engine today.'

Then came the words I was hoping to hear.

'You two can take the small boat and go diving if you want to.'

We immediately stopped the teasing and started to plan where we would dive. Over the past few weeks, we'd become an expert team.

Solomon stuck his head around the corner of the bar.

'My job's done,' he said, as he strolled over to our table. 'Chairs and umbrellas are out. Grandpa will be here soon. He's always quick to take money from anyone who wants to use them.'

'Hey Sol, wanna come diving?' Jack had spoken after he'd taken his last mouthful of bacon bap, and tomato sauce started to dribble down his chin and on to his tee shirt. I smiled and passed him a paper serviette.

What ... this morning? Yeah, great.' Solomon grinned his biggest grin. 'Is it okay with you, Dan?' he asked. 'Can I borrow some dive equipment too?'

'Yes, of course, and I'm trusting you all to dive sensibly and not take risks,' said Dan, 'so look after each other. You're my super buddy team of three, okay?'

'We'll be fine, Dan!' said Jack. 'Stop worrying, we're all experts at diving now.'

'I agree,' said Dan, 'you're all good divers ... but problems can sometimes creep up on you when you're least expecting them. One minute everything's fine, then next minute you're looking at a disaster.'

I later thought back to that conversation, and wondered if Dan had the powers of premonition?'

Could he have known what would happen ... that later in the day our lives *would* be in real danger?

CHAPTER TWENTY-FIVE

Rocky Reef

We collected our dive kit and took the rigid inflatable boat half-a-mile out from Dolphin Beach. Slowing as we approached the marker buoy for Rocky Reef, Solomon stopped the engine and Jack tied the boat to the buoy. We soon had our dive kit on and sat on the cushioned sides of the boat.

'We'll have to keep an eye on the weather,' I said. 'Looks like storm clouds over there.' I could feel the wind blowing harder and watched a lone gull swooping in the sky.

'That'll soon blow over,' said Jack. 'We don't get many storms at this time of year. We're gonna be safe and snug underwater anyhow.'

'Ready?' I asked. I got okay signs back from Jack and Sol and signed a thumbs-down signal. We all rolled back, splashed into the water and slowly descended twenty-five metres.

A shoal of docile spadefish slowly swam past, their large bodies shimmering in the sunlight breaking through from the surface. I counted over twenty of them as I hung in the water letting them cross in front of me. Blue fusiliers, in a shoal of what must have been over a hundred identical fish, flashed the narrow black and white stripes on the side of their bodies as they moved through the water.

Jack pointed to our left. I watched as a black-tipped reef shark swam purposefully alongside us, about five metres away. No worries. Reef sharks don't attack humans, but I watched it carefully anyway as it swam away from us, minding its own business. It was streamlined and awesome and perfectly suited for its underwater life. We were so lucky to see such a gorgeous animal in the wild.

We swam closer to the reef wall, which was covered in bright, gloriously coloured soft corals. There were purple, pink and white coral tentacles grasping outwards in the water, catching nearly invisible plankton and pushing the food into their central mouth cavities. The tentacles moved in the water, like a choir opening and closing their mouths to sing. The silent rhythm of their movement being conducted by an invisible choirmaster.

We drifted alongside the reef wall passing an enormous fan coral. Tiny sea slugs were creeping along its branches. I remembered Joel telling me that these impressive corals were often over five hundred years old.

As we swam towards an outcrop of hard coral, a brown and white patterned hawkfish emerged from the coral close to my face. The fish had been camouflaged by the similar colours on its body which matched the reef. I knew it couldn't hurt me, but I was surprised by its sudden movement.

A shy, little puffer fish turned away from us and hid in a crevice. A wart slug crawled slowly over a prickly piece of staghorn coral, its orange and black striped, bumpy skin showing up clearly against the pale coloured hard coral.

Then I saw we had a serious problem. One of the air hoses attached to Jack's tank was leaking and air bubbles were racing to the surface.

I signalled to Sol to stay close to me. Jack couldn't see the escaping bubbles for himself as the tank was on his back, but I could see the danger.

Was Jack's tank leaking slowly or was the valve about to blow? Sometimes a valve could become worn and suddenly, with no warning, it would explode, creating a loud bang and releasing a fierce bubble stream of pressurised gas from the tank. The sudden rush of air bubbles from a valve failure was so strong it could knock a mouthpiece out of a diver's mouth and leave them struggling for air.

If the valve did blow, Jack was in danger of losing his whole air supply in seconds.

Could I swim across and tighten the valve from behind him? My touching it might cause the valve to disintegrate and blow ... straight into my face and so endangering my own life.

It was a big risk but there was no question in my mind. I had to go and help him.

How much air was Jack losing? How much air did he have left? Would he be able to get to the surface safely?

I had to make a quick decision. I came up behind him and pulled on his shoulder to turn him around to face me. I wobbled my hand to signal 'problem.'

The eyes behind his mask were questioning and I tried to explain with my hands about the leak. He nodded, but I wasn't sure if he'd understood the danger. I asked him to show me his air gauge. We needed to know how much air he had left in his tank.

Jack looked horrified when he saw his tank was nearly empty. There was no point in me trying to adjust the valve, he'd hardly any air left in his tank. I decided to concentrate on getting Jack back up to the surface as fast as I could.

I signalled to Sol to surface with us and held on to Jack's buoyancy jacket. We kicked our fins to go upwards and stayed close to each other. I prepared to give Jack my spare air hose. He'd be able to share the air in my tank by breathing through it. But that, of course, would mean that my air supply would then reduce twice as fast. We could soon both be without an air supply.

My depth gauge was reading twenty metres. I looked up. We'd got a long way to go before we reached safety at the surface.

CHAPTER TWENTY-SIX

Different Worlds

Halfway to the surface, Jack's air supply ran out and he reached for my spare mouthpiece and hose. I gave him the okay signal and held him close to me. His breathing was fast. He was obviously nervous. My spare hose was working well but Jack was using up our shared air quite quickly.

When we reached five metres from the surface, Sol signalled for us all to do a three-minute safety stop. Three minutes felt like a very long time to wait as we hung in the water and watched our wrist computers tick down.

My air gauge told me we were nearly out of air. With two of us breathing from the same tank we'd almost used it all up. There was nothing I could do but wait for the time to tick away. It was dangerous for us to ignore a safety stop and return to the surface too quickly, but would the air in our tank last for long enough? I daren't look at Jack in case he saw how frightened I was.

Then Sol spun around and gave us the 'okay to surface' signal.

I expected our heads to emerge into warm bright sunlight, with gentle waves splashing over our faces, but the world we'd left at the surface had changed. Heavy clouds had formed, stopping the warm sun from reaching down. The wind had increased, and big waves were making it difficult to swim to our boat.

Sol reached the rubber rigid inflatable boat first and pulled himself in. He removed his tank and fins quickly, then helped both Jack and me into the RIB.

'Wow, that was a bit scary,' said Jack. Jack for once, was not joking or messing about. He let out a big sigh. 'I was very close to panicking,' he said, 'I couldn't even remember why we had to do the safety stop. I wanted to rush straight to the surface. Then I remembered Dan telling us about poisonous nitrogen gas and how it builds up in our bodies when we dive deep. We could have died from decompression sickness if we hadn't stopped at five metres.'

'I was scared too, Jack,' I admitted, 'I was terrified when I saw the air level so low in the tank we were sharing. Those three minutes, waiting to get to the surface ... they felt like three hours!'

'Thanks though, Lucy,' he said. 'If you hadn't noticed those bubbles leaking out … hey, I could have totally run out of air when we were further apart. It was scary enough having to share your air tank when we were close together. It was an awful feeling when my air ran out. I don't think I'd have made it back to the surface if you hadn't helped me.'

'No problem,' I said. I was probably sounding braver than I felt.

Jack was still shaking. 'It was totally scary!'

'We sorted it out between us, so that's good,' I said, 'but I think we're all a bit shocked.'

'Didn't help that the weather was rubbish when we reached the surface,' said Sol, 'it made it more difficult to get into the boat.'

'Typical,' said Jack, 'that storm's blown over now ... sun's out again.'

We sat back in the RIB letting the sun warm our bodies.

That's better,' I said, my eyes closing. '... more peaceful now.'

'I think we've worked well as a buddy team again today,' said Jack, 'that problem was serious.'

'We've been lucky today, too.' said Sol. 'If the wind had been stronger our RIB might've broken loose from the buoy ... we could have surfaced and found there was no boat to get us back!'

I opened my eyes.

'Actually, this morning's been perfect,' I said.

Jack and Sol stared at me.

'What ARE you talking about, Lucy? It was really dangerous,' said Sol.

'Yes, I know, but I've just been thinking about our friend the turtle and how we both live in such different worlds. Think about it ... underwater is an alien world for us. We need our air supply, and we need to look after each other. When it seems all calm down below, it can be blowing a gale up here on the surface ... in our real world.'

'Well, turtles are streamlined and swim easily in the water ... and storms don't affect them,' said Jack.

'I'm still not sure what you mean, Lucy,' said Sol. 'Why was this morning so useful to you?'

'I suppose I'm trying to say that we mustn't treat the sea creatures as if they were living in our world, either. They don't. Our two worlds are alien to each other. '

'Well, most people don't dive like we do, so I suppose they can't imagine what it's like,' said Jack.

'Exactly,' I said, 'people don't understand how these creatures live and survive. They don't see the vastness of the space where these animals swim. Joel was telling me that dolphins swim up to a hundred miles a day in the open water of the oceans, yet people build sea world theme parks and put those beautiful creatures in small swimming pools.'

Jack looked sad. 'Those dolphins must really suffer.'

'It's like putting them in cages, just so humans can look at them?' said Sol.

'Exactly,' I said. 'Today might've been a bit scary for us,' I said, 'but it's made me realise even more that most people don't understand the oceans at all.'

CHAPTER TWENTY-SEVEN

Snorkelling at Dolphin Beach

When we returned to the Dive Centre, I chatted with Dan about how the valve could've got twisted.

'It probably mis-threaded when Jack put his hose on the tank,' said Dan, 'I'll talk with him before you all dive again and check that he's sure about how to do it properly.'

Dan squeezed my shoulder.

'You did well to deal with the problem, Lucy, and you did the right thing to get the boys and yourself straight back to the surface.'

'It was a shame it happened, as it was beautiful down there this morning ... there was so much going on.'

'And you still haven't seen a scary sea monster,' he said, laughing.

'Yeah, I know swimming scared me for so long didn't it, but not anymore.'

'Mmmm,' said Dan, 'you did well to stay calm and get everyone back safely, but it was a serious moment. Diving is a dangerous thing to do. Even when it's tranquil and beautiful underwater, you always need to be aware of the dangers around you.'

I listened carefully, but I was determined. I was going to continue diving, however hazardous it was, and I was going to use my understanding of the underwater world to help me look after the sea creatures.

I thought of Joel and smiled. When he'd said that understanding the sea would change my life, he'd been right ... by learning to dive I'd begun to understand the world where sea creatures lived.

We rinsed and tidied our equipment away before we asked Dan if we could borrow masks and snorkels. Our plan was to investigate the reef near the beach to see how much litter had collected there.

'No problem,' said Dan, 'just don't frighten the sea creatures when they see your ugly face looking down at them, Jack.'

Dan turned and winked at me.

'Hey, Uncle Dan, stop picking on me.'

'Dan's just telling the truth, Jack,' I said.

'Uhm, stop ganging up on me!' said Jack, as he pretended to be upset.

The three of us were soon snorkelling. We drifted on the surface, in a gentle current, on a calm sea. There was hardly a breeze, so no waves disturbed the water and we could see clearly down to the reef. The scene below us was beautiful and my eyes were busy trying to find animals I'd not seen before, but my tranquillity was soon shattered. I could see plastic bottles caught up in the crevices and plastic straws and bags floating in the water.

I raised my head above the water.

'The amount of litter on this reef is terrible,' I said, 'how can those poor animals live in all that rubbish?' Jack and Sol raised their heads from the water when they heard me speak.

'It's awful. I've never seen it that bad before,' said Sol, 'it seems to be getting worse.'

As we walked back up the beach, I saw Joel drinking his afternoon cup of tea at Drifters.

'Joel, can I ask you something?' I said. 'We need to start doing something to help the sea creatures. We've just seen the most terrible amount of rubbish all over the reef out there.'

'Yep, and look at the beach,' said Solomon, 'it's covered in litter underneath the chairs I put out this morning. The holidaymakers are still dropping stuff from their picnics. There's plastic water bottles and food wrappers everywhere.'

Joel was nodding. 'That's the trouble with people,' he said, 'they leave their rubbish behind everywhere, then it gets swept out by the breeze into the sea.'

'And plastic bags get caught in the mouths of turtles,' I said, quietly. 'I wish there was something we could do to make everyone realise how much harm they're all doing.'

'Well, let's brainstorm,' said Jack, 'we must be able to come up with some ideas.'

We sat down around Joel's table.

'Joel, do you remember telling me that learning to dive would help me understand about the life in the sea?'

'Yes, I remember that,' said Joel.

'Well, I think this morning, it all got straightened out in my head and I began to understand more about how our two worlds are so different.'

'Yeah, there are two worlds ... the underwater world and the world that humans live in, right?' said Jack.

'That's it, Jack ... think about it,' I said, 'all humans understand about living on land. They understand their own lives in cities, and they understand land animals, so animals like elephants and pandas get protected, but people rarely see what it's like underwater, so they don't understand how these creatures live or what they need to survive.'

'I suppose most people don't even think about what it's like in the ocean,' said Sol.

'That's right, Sol,' I said, 'because they don't see it for themselves. If they throw litter in the sea, they probably think it all disappears 'cos they can't see it anymore.'

Sol was nodding.

'That's what I think I've understood today ... just how different our two worlds are. Somehow, we've got to help people understand how all this plastic rubbish is ruining the underwater world. If elephants had to tip-toe between plastic trash then there'd be headlines on TV every day and people would be making a fuss, but because it's happening in the ocean, no-one sees the problems.'

Jack and Sol were nodding thoughtfully.

'So, it's about ignorance, isn't it?' I said. 'If people haven't seen how beautiful the reef is, or they have no idea what amazing creatures are living in the sea, then they won't understand the dangers of dropping litter and allowing it to get in the water.'

'That's right,' said Joel. 'These holiday people don't think there's much happening in the sea, at all. They've got no idea. When they go swimming, they splash about and frighten all the fish away, so when they look down, they don't see much life down there at all. They don't keep still like you and I do when we snorkel. They don't just look down quietly and watch the wildlife.'

'So, you're saying that these people just don't know what's living out there,' said Jack, 'and probably haven't got a clue about what's happening to their litter either.'

Joel was nodding.

'Yes, Jack,' said Joel, 'that's it exactly. They probably don't understand that plastic stays in the ocean for hundreds of years, either.'

CHAPTER TWENTY-EIGHT

Make a Difference

'We need to educate people, the same as I've learnt all about it since I moved here,' I said. 'If we could share what we know with locals and people on holiday, then it's bound to make a difference. They'll want to look after the sea creatures just as much as we do.'

'But I don't know how we can do that,' said Solomon. 'How can we teach them about the sea?'

'Pick 'em up off those sunbeds and throw 'em in!' said Jack, 'then they'll see the rubbish for themselves.' He was glaring at the holidaymakers.

Jack turned to see us all staring at him. Had he been listening to anything we'd talked about?

'Yeah, okay, so I'm kidding. That's not a proper idea at all, is it?'

'No, Jack,' said Joel, 'we have to get people interested sensibly.'

'Look,' I said, 'we've all read Dan's fish identification books and guides, but the holidaymakers aren't likely to read those, they're too busy reading their books of murders and horror stories. How about if we give them something different to read, with beautiful pictures of the animals alongside it? We could have big boards ... with lots of information that people could come and read.'

'What sort of things are you suggesting for these boards, Lucy?' asked Solomon.

'Well, I suppose pictures of the animals ... like a beautiful turtle photo and then tell everyone the facts about turtles. We could do that for lots of the creatures, not just turtles, but stingrays, butterfly fish and others, like the parrotfish and even the tiniest of sea slugs. People would love to look at pictures of all those, wouldn't they? We know loads of interesting facts about the way these creatures live. I'm sure they'd get interested too.'

'It sounds like you've hit on a good idea there, Lucy,' said Joel, 'information boards would be great, but they need to be made of strong stuff, so they can last for ages, and the information has to look good and be printed with everything in colour.'

'And we could tell them about the dangerous things they have to look out for,' said Jack, 'like jellyfish or things that're poisonous. Everyone should learn about all that too.'

'The boards would probably need to be covered in glass or something, to protect them,' said Solomon, 'and we'd need quite a few of them along the beach.'

'If we put them at the edge of the beach near the road, then locals walking along the footpath could read them, as well,' I said.

'These are all good ideas, Lucy,' said Joel. 'I'm sure there are loads of people who live on Pontus, who don't swim much and don't dive, and they need to know about not dropping litter too.'

'And we need litter bins,' I said, 'and signs to encourage everyone to put their litter in bins and not let it all blow around the beach ... and we need to show pictures of what is happening to the animals too. Pictures like our turtle with the plastic bag in its mouth, or pictures of the reef covered in plastic bottles. If we show it all, then I'm sure people would be horrified about what's happening.'

'Problem is, Lucy,' said Joel, 'these are all great ideas but it's not just this beach, it's every beach on Pontus Island that needs information.'

'Of course, Joel, I hadn't thought of that,' I said, 'There's no point in doing just one beach is there? You're right, it's the whole of Pontus and all the sea around it that we need to fight for.'

Mmm ... the ideas were crashing around inside my skull and my brain started to ache. 'If we're going to do all this then we need a plan. We have to organise it all properly.'

'But hold on, Lucy,' said Joel, 'there's something else you're not thinking about ... and that's the cost of doing all this. Making the boards won't be cheap if they're made to last ... and none of us has any money to achieve all this.'

'Yeah, Lucy, I don't think we can do all this, can we?' said Jack. 'I can't see how we can do anything by ourselves.'

'Well, I'm going to find a way,' I said, 'I'm not sure how we're going to do it, but I made a promise to my turtle friend and I'm not giving up on it.'

CHAPTER TWENTY-NINE

Pirates' Peak

I saw Dan heading for us. 'I thought you were all snorkelling?' he said.

We explained about the litter and the ideas we'd been discussing.

'Problem is,' said Joel, 'we need to find a way of getting money to do everything.'

'Umm, I might have an idea,' said Dan. 'I've got a friend who lives up on Pirates' Peak Hill. I met her ages ago when she used to dive. She used to work in a big university, teaching marine biology, up on the west coast of America, then came to live here a few years ago. She'd certainly understand how the animals in the sea are suffering and what it is you're trying to do here. She might have some contacts or know how to raise some money for your ideas.'

'She sounds interesting, Dan,' said Joel, 'perhaps you and Lucy can go and talk to her.'

Dan got out his phone and I soon heard him talking to his friend.

'Okay, that'll be great. Yep, we'll see you in the morning. Bye.'

He turned to me smiling.

'She's expecting us at ten o'clock tomorrow. That's fine by me as I've got no-one booked in to dive, so I'll meet you at quarter to ten. It doesn't take long to drive up to her house. I haven't seen her for ages, so it'll be good for me to catch up with all her news.'

I really hoped this lady would have some ideas that could help us, but I shivered at the thought of meeting someone new. I told myself to trust Dan's judgement about people, this lady would probably be okay ... but my imagination decided to work overtime and planted a picture in my head of a boring, old woman who spoke stuffily about scientific things I didn't understand and who would make me feel I was just a kid with stupid ideas. I didn't sleep well that night, as my dreams were haunted by a wicked old witch from a child's story book.

In the morning, Dan drove us both in his old 4x4, which was covered in adverts for the Dive Centre.

We went east, which was new to me, as the bus to St. Stephens and school always took me away from Jude's Bay to the west. As we drove through the next two villages, I was reminded of how poor some of the islanders were. The scruffy houses I'd seen when I'd arrived on Pontus were still alongside the roads, but there were no properties that seemed to have had any recent hurricane damage. There were fewer houses to be seen as we took the road up towards a higher part of the island. As the car twisted and turned around the narrow bends, I could look out across the tops of the trees and see the sea below, sparkling in the distance.

'They call this area Pirates' Peak,' said Dan, 'because in the olden days they kept watch for pirates from up here and could get early warning of ships coming close to the island.'

Dan slowed the car and turned through tall gates onto a drive, taking us up to an old house with a large balcony. The garden had colourful flowers, but they looked bashed about and were no longer standing upright.

'The wind gets quite strong up here,' said Dan. 'It must be a bit of a battle to keep the garden tidy in this wind and Ellen must struggle a bit. She's told me she finds some things difficult these days, as her old bones don't let her do everything she wants. That's why she doesn't dive anymore.' He parked the car. 'Come on, you'll like her. She knows so much about sea creatures.'

I gently knocked on the door but jumped as I heard dogs barking. Did the wicked witch in my dreams have large monstrous dogs that would snarl and snap at my ankles?

When the door was thrown open, I saw a small lady, who was bent over, trying to hold onto the collars of two friendly dogs. She had frizzy, ginger hair and freckles positioned around her face like splattered brown paint spots. The skin around her face was creased, with small lines like birds' footsteps in the sand, surrounding her hazel-green eyes. What I hadn't imagined was her wonderfully friendly and smiley face.

Had this woman really been a scientist and a diver? She looked like a little old grandma and was nothing like the images I'd had in my dreams.

'Oh, come in, come in,' she said. 'My name's Ellen. Don't mind the boys, they're just pleased to see you. No! Charlie. Don't jump up. I hope they don't frighten you, Lucy. Albert's the quiet one, he's got too old to jump up, but Charlie's still only a puppy and he'll want to play with you.'

Once the door was closed, Ellen let go of the dogs and they ran excitedly around my legs. My ankles seemed safe; these were not the monsters I'd dreamt of all night.

'You've learnt to dive already, I hear. That's brilliant. I used to dive when I was younger.'

Ellen gave Dan a hug. 'Come on in then, Dan. Do you want some tea or coffee?'

Ellen was asking me questions about London whilst she made the tea, then carried the cups and cookies to the balcony at the back of the house. The view was amazing. I could look far out to sea. No pirates, today though.

'My job in America included research on whale behaviour,' said Ellen. 'It was very exciting. When I retired, I promised myself I'd find a home where I could see the sea every day and I love living here on Pontus.'

I understood why Dan had continued to be her friend. As we sat talking, I relaxed. I felt comfortable in this lady's company. She'd made me feel welcome and we had so much in common. I loved the fact that she'd been a diver. She knew so much about the turtles, stingrays and all my favourite sea creatures.

When she asked about the ideas we'd had to help prevent litter in the ocean she was very encouraging. I felt I could respect her opinions.

'Yes, you are so right about educating everyone,' she said. 'Education is behind everything we need to do. Not many people understand, especially if they don't dive like you or Dan. I fully understand why you want to protect the sea life.'

But then she added words I didn't want to hear.

'Trouble is, you've got some big obstacles in your way.'

CHAPTER THIRTY

Tell the World

'I do love your ideas about information boards,' Ellen was saying, 'and of course, we must have lots more litter bins and signs to remind people to put their rubbish in them too, but we'll need to convince the Pontus Island officials that it all needs doing and persuade them to fund it all.'

I exchanged glances with Dan. He was looking worried.

'We'll also need people to do the artwork, get the facts right, organise the pictures, make it look really good, and we have to make strong wooden or metal frames,' said Ellen. 'Lucy, there is so much involved. It's not going to be easy at all!'

I tried to add something positive.

'I was thinking last night,' I said, 'that perhaps I could ask to run a competition at school, by getting pupils to design 'Don't Drop Litter' and 'Bin It' signs. I've only ever seen boring signs back in London, and we need to have more imaginative ideas if we're to draw attention to them.'

'That's a good idea,' said Ellen, 'it'll get the local community involved too, so we can add that to the list but we need the bins first and it also gives you another problem, as you'll need a sponsor who could pay for a prize. Maybe a sponsor could pay for the finished signs too.'

'But let's be positive. We can try to get some sponsorship,' said Ellen, 'and I think we might get local people involved in this. We need people to use their voices to demand something is done and get someone in the local Council who can organise it all.'

She was thinking quietly, staring out to sea. 'Actually, I do know someone who works for the Council. I think he's in the planning office, but he might be useful to us. So, while you're eating all the cookies, I'll get on the phone to him, right now.'

She rushed inside and left us on the balcony.

Albert had fallen asleep wrapped around Dan's ankles, whilst Charlie sat close to my feet, his head on my knee, scrutinizing every move I made as I ate my cookie. His eyes, emerging from under tufts of hairy eyebrows, watched for any dropped crumbs.

'Sorry, Charlie,' I said, 'but I'm not leaving any crumbs for you. I'm sure you're not supposed to eat these chocolate chips anyway.'

Ellen wasn't gone for long and she was looking downright miserable. 'Well, that wasn't very successful,' she said. 'I spoke with Roger. He says he's sympathetic about what we're talking about but feels he wouldn't get support from the Council. He was quite dismissive, saying most people wouldn't think it was important to their life on Pontus Island.'

'But sea creatures are important,' I said. 'He just doesn't understand, does he?'

'This is what we're up against, Lucy,' said Ellen. 'Peoples' ignorance. He doesn't understand what we're worrying about. He said the Council is too busy mending roads and making sure the buses run on time.'

I looked at Dan. He was looking disappointed.

'It doesn't sound like our plans are going to happen,' he said. 'I was really hoping that Lucy's ideas would get some support.'

131

'There's a lot of truth in what Roger thinks,' said Ellen, 'but, he did offer one idea. He said that if we could supply some evidence for what we say is happening, things like the plastic on the reefs and animals getting caught up in plastic bags and so on, then he will put it forward to a committee he works with.'

I quietly sat and tickled Charlie's head.

'I suppose we could send them a photo of the bags of rubbish we collect every time we clean up the beach,' I said. 'Would that be enough?'

Ellen jumped to her feet. 'That's it, Lucy, you've got it! Photos! And I think I might have an answer to that,' said Ellen. 'I've still got my underwater camera. I'll get it, and you can take it diving with you. You can take photographs and video and get evidence of all the rubbish. Then we can show it to the Council.'

She went rushing off again and soon returned with a bag full of exciting things ... a camera, an underwater case, some filters, a gadget to clip the camera case onto a diver's jacket and lots of other bits and pieces to do with keeping the camera clean and ensuring the case didn't leak.

'It's easy to use, I'll show you,' said Ellen. 'The video has a simple on and off switch and a zoom, so you can record close up too.'

Ellen explained how to change the memory card and download it on to a computer.

'You can use my computer, Lucy,' said Dan, 'as soon as you've got some film to download.'

'Thanks, Dan.' I said, 'that's brilliant. If we film the evidence, we can show it to people who might help us.'

'We're relying on you now, Lucy,' said Ellen. 'Find something that'll prove we need to help these creatures.'

As we drove back to Jude's Bay I sat quietly in the car. Ellen had challenged me to get the evidence and we would have a battle to convince people, but I recalled our turtle rescue. I might have to fight harder than I'd thought for what I believed in, but I wasn't ready to give up yet.

CHAPTER THIRTY-ONE

Evidence Needed

'Wow,' said Jack, 'this is some bit of kit. We'll need to put the underwater case on properly, or the camera could get flooded and it won't ever work again. We should double check it every time we use it.'

'Triple-check it, probably,' said Sol. 'I'd hate to be the one who got it wrong.'

We all agreed to learn how to use it and carried it down with us to the water's edge, but soon found that trying to film whilst we were snorkelling at the surface was almost impossible.

'This is hopeless,' I said, 'there are only a few waves but they're pushing me around on the surface. I can't keep the camera still at all.'

'Let me try.' said Jack. 'Ah, I see what you mean. It's pathetic.'

Sol tried too. 'It's not only that we can't keep it still,' he said, 'but we're too far away up on the surface. We need to get closer to the reef.'

'Let's find Dan,' I said, 'even though we don't need to go very deep, we need to get dive equipment, go down and stay down there to video things.'

'This looks like trouble.' Dan looked up as we all stomped into the equipment room together.

Jack explained our need to borrow dive equipment. 'But we won't need to use a boat, Dan,' he said, 'we can just walk in off the beach.'

134

'We need to practise handling the camera and see if we can record the rubbish we've seen on the reef,' said Sol.

'Practise this afternoon,' said Dan, 'then bring the camera back here so we can all see what video you get.'

We pulled on the kit and walked back down the beach. We only had to dive five metres to see the reef more clearly. As I took my turn, I found myself absorbed in the challenge of recording the scene in front of us. The fish were constantly  swimming away from me. So, plenty of film of fishy tails to choose from, but then I remembered we were supposed to be filming the plastic on the reef, not the fish. I found the real task much easier as the coral and plastic bottles didn't move.

We took turns using the camera, then headed for the Dive Centre and crowded around the computer screen.

'Look, there's the little puffer fish, going to hide in the coral,' I said, 'and you see those butterfly fish, they're so beautiful. It's great. I love it. It's like doing the dive all over again.'

'We could do with a bit more practice, though,' said Jack. 'I was still shaking a lot when I filmed the plastic bottles in the staghorn coral. I need to learn how to keep the camera steady.'

'My effort was terrible,' said Solomon. 'I tried filming a parrotfish eating algae off the coral next to some plastic and all I got was the fish's tail. I hadn't filmed its head or the plastic at all.'

'Well, we can't expect to be brilliant straight away,' I said.

Dan overheard us and came over.

'I expect you'll soon get the hang of it,' he said. 'Why don't you practise after school next week, then next weekend, take the RIB to go further out where it's deeper. You'll find more creatures to film out there, and I'd like to know how much plastic there is out in the deeper water anyway.'

'I'll be kind to you, Lucy,' he said. 'You can have a week off from restocking the shop. Go and dive together in the afternoons to practise with the camera, and when you've finished you can all help Solomon bring in the chairs. That'll keep Joel happy too.'

'Thanks, Dan,' I said. 'If we improve during the week, then at the weekend we can try hard to get some really good film.'

CHAPTER THIRTY-TWO

Camera Work

When Saturday dawned, I jumped out of bed and ran to the Dive Centre. We carried our kit down to the RIB and sped off across the bay.

Our plan was to spend our day filming at the outer edge of the local reef, so we triple-checked the camera and fitted a red filter to record the colour in the deeper water. We had practised all week so were more confident of holding the camera still and taking good shots.

We splashed in and dropped to twenty metres, the reef appearing below us and getting closer.

Jack and Sol took turns in filming ripped plastic packaging, old plastic food containers, cling film and cotton buds.

When it was my turn to use the camera, I swam down to an area of coral near the seabed. Jack was close by and I pointed out a crab, walking along the sand. Suddenly, I saw it had a flat piece of plastic food tray around its leg. The crab must have punctured the plastic tray with its pincer and now it was stuck, unable to get it off. It looked like it was wearing a large, cumbersome, plastic bracelet.

I filmed the creature trying to walk and wondered how long the plastic had been hindering the crab's ability to catch food and feed itself. I stopped filming, attached the camera on its clip to my jacket and let it float beside me. Then, I went to help the crab.

Okay, little chap, stay still, I'll help you. I got hold of the creature around its shell, keeping my fingers well away from its pincers. I pulled at the plastic but couldn't get it loose.

Jack came to help me, and as I held the crab, he used both hands to remove the plastic tray.

Yep, it's off. I cheered inwardly and turned to Jack, so we could exchange a high-five. I could see his smiley eyes behind his mask. Sol joined in.

Mission accomplished. One rescued crab and a lot of video. We all checked our air. Thirty minutes left. I signalled to move further along the reef.

It was then I heard it. A clicking noise. I turned to look all around me. There was nothing close by us. I looked upwards. A pod of five dolphins were swimming above us. I couldn't believe I was seeing dolphins for the first time. They were magnificent creatures and so streamlined. A perfect body shape for fast swimming. My excitement was bubbling over as I watched them.

The dolphins were clicking loudly. There was one small dolphin in the centre of the group. Two of the bigger dolphins were underneath it, pushing it to the surface.

I remembered dolphins were marine mammals. They needed to go to the surface to breathe air and supply their bodies with oxygen.

Why were these dolphins having to lift the little one to the surface? Was it a baby, still learning how to breathe, or was there a problem? We slowly kicked our fins to go up and investigate.

As we got closer, I saw the young dolphin was in trouble. It was covered in a damaged plastic fishing net. The netting was caught tightly against its body and it couldn't move its fins or open its mouth. It couldn't swim to the surface by itself, so the older, bigger dolphins were working together to push the youngster up to the surface at regular intervals to keep it alive.

As we moved up through the water, I started filming. I swam around the group, taking film and trying to think about how we could help.

CHAPTER THIRTY-THREE

Dolphin in Trouble

Jack and Sol were close by. Jack took his dive knife out of its holder and signalled to Sol to do the same. As they swam towards the dolphins the clicking got louder. Two of the large dolphins moved further away. They seemed to understand that Jack and Sol needed space to get closer.

Jack swam to the young dolphin and tried to pull at the fishing net, but it was so tight he couldn't move it. He took a small piece in his hand and carefully cut it. Sol saw what he was doing and went around the other side to do the same.

They were cutting the fishing net away as quickly as they could, then one of the older dolphins came and nudged Jack's knee.

Jack stopped cutting and moved away from the young dolphin. He signalled to Sol to do the same.

As they moved back, two of the larger dolphins came underneath and lifted the youngster up to the surface. When the young dolphin had taken some breaths of air, they allowed it to sink below the surface again and moved away, allowing Jack and Sol to continue cutting the net.

It was going to take some time, but Jack, Sol and the dolphins started to work as a team, with Jack and Sol stopping the cutting every time the biggest dolphin touched Jack's knee.

I was filming all the time. I couldn't believe we were able to help these creatures.

Checking my dive watch I saw we'd only got ten minutes of air left. I hoped they'd get the dolphin free soon.

Jack and Sol were just pulling away to allow the dolphin to be pushed to the surface once more when I realised there was a problem. A large lump of the old fishing net, which had been cut away from the dolphin, was floating in the water, and Sol had just backed into it.

The netting was caught around Sol's head and getting tighter the more he struggled.

Jack saw the problem and quickly swam to Sol. He attacked the net with his knife, but he pulled on the net too quickly, and he ripped Sol's mask from his face.

Sol started to panic ... his arms were flailing around, and he accidentally hit Jack in the face.

They were now both getting caught up in the netting as Sol was still panicking and Jack, still dazed after being hit, backed into another lump of the plastic net.

The camera floated beside me as I quickly swam towards them. Sol was now without his mask. It had fallen around the back of his tank and caught in the netting, but he couldn't reach it. The netting was trapping his arms, tight to his body.

I reached for his mask and tried to get it back on his head, but without Sol being able to use his hands to help, it kept slipping off and it was impossible for me to get it back on his face. I tucked the mask safely in my belt, signalled 'stay calm', then got my own knife out.

Only five more minutes of air was left. Were Jack and Sol going to be trapped by this net and be unable to get back to the surface before their air ran out? Were any of us going to be able to get to the surface safely?

Slashing at the net, I pulled it away as quickly as I could. When Sol was free, I handed him his mask, then raced over to Jack. The net had got caught up around his air hoses. I had to be doubly careful as I cut it away. If his air supply was cut ... then he'd be in even worse trouble.

Sol went back to work on the young dolphin and managed to get it completely free.

I eventually got Jack clear of the net, but he was still stunned and confused. Although everyone was now clear, we only had a few minutes of air left. I signed to Jack and Sol.

UP!

But Sol was trying to signal something else. I didn't understand. What did he want me to do?

He was collecting the netting carefully, pulling it all together near his tummy, away from his face and air hoses. Now, I understood. Signalling 'okay' and pointing to myself, I signalled UP.

I grabbed Jack and pulled him up to the surface. Once he was in the fresh air he revived quickly and he was able to get into the RIB.

'Stay here,' I said, 'help Sol and me get the plastic netting into the boat.'

There was hardly any air left in my tank. Decision time. Stay safe on the boat in the air or go down again and make sure Sol was safe.

My decision was instant. I had to risk running out of air to help Sol and make sure he got to the surface safely, but we wouldn't be able to stay down for long.

The dolphins were circling us at a distance. They were still communicating with each other with clicks.

We collected chunks of net, then took it up to the RIB for Jack to pull safely onboard, then went back for more. We made three more trips to the boat with netting.

Then ... the dolphins joined in. I knew they were intelligent creatures and I'd seen a television programme showing them playing together. Did they think it was a game? Maybe they understood we were cleaning up the ocean. They were swimming towards pieces of floating net, catching it on their noses and taking it up to Jack.

Jack got a shock the first time a dolphin surfaced alongside me as I was delivering netting to the boat, but soon realised he had to take the net off the dolphin's nose.

Only a few seconds left. I dived again. Pulling at the cable of the camera so it floated towards me. I began to film. The dolphins were swimming around Sol, collecting loose pieces of netting and helping him take it up to Jack. Wow, what a scene.

Then ... my air ran out! I was sucking at the mouthpiece but there was no air coming through. Did my lungs contain enough air to get me back to the surface?

My wrist computer bleeped loudly ... a warning ... air tank empty!

Okay, I know! I was pleased we were so shallow in the water that we didn't need to do a safety stop.

I signalled to Sol and managed to hold my breath until we reached the surface.

As my lungs were filling with fresh air, Jack pulled me, then Sol, into the boat. It was packed with plastic netting. I started to film again, taking shots of the dolphins appearing at the surface with more net and Jack talking to the dolphins as they surrounded the boat.

'Thanks, buddy, well done,' he said, and patted one on the nose.

I couldn't believe what had happened. Dan had warned us that diving was hazardous and this time, running out of air had put our lives in real danger, but the risk had been worth it. Our efforts had been rewarded and we had the evidence we'd been hoping for.

CHAPTER THIRTY-FOUR

Captured on Camera

When Dan realised what incredible film we'd recorded, he couldn't stop talking.

'You've got video evidence of the damage that's happening in the ocean, and the way the dolphins helped to clear up the netting is utterly astonishing.'

He phoned Mum to tell her to come and see the film and asked Sol to get his grandpa over too. He phoned Ellen, and she drove down from Pirates' Peak.

The film clips of the net trapping Sol and Jack and the dolphins helping us was loved by everyone. We were all celebrating.

'This is the evidence we needed,' said Ellen. 'Well done, Lucy ... and Jack and Sol, you've all done so well.'

Ellen offered to do a proper editing job on the film, and we discussed what our next move should be.

'Well, once it's edited,' said Ellen, 'we can contact Roger and let him see it too. I think this proves everything we said about our worries about plastic. Surely no-one will turn down our ideas now.'

'I've been thinking about that too,' I said, 'and I think I've got another argument too. Do you remember that your council friend said that no-one would be interested, as the ocean wasn't important enough? Well, I think the problem is not just about the cleaning up the ocean for the sea animals.'

What do you mean?' asked Dan.

'Have the politicians thought about the money the island gets from the people on holiday? Don't those holidaymakers come to sit and look at a wonderfully clean, blue sea? If we let the ocean water around the Island become a giant litter collection area, then no-one would want to come here. The money they bring into the island must pay for lots of things on Pontus, like schools and hospitals. We need the politicians to think about all this. If the tourists don't come, then the island could become poor ... it could be disastrous for Pontus.

'Yes, you're spot on, Lucy,' said Ellen, 'we need to make sure the arguments for stopping litter getting in the ocean are heard. It's so important for everyone, the Government, the locals and the folk who travel here for their holidays.'

'And for the animals too,' said Sol.

'Yeah', said Jack. 'We can't be there to help turtles and dolphins all the time, can we? There must a load of creatures who are suffering without anyone knowing.'

'Like that little crab,' said Sol. 'How long had he been wearing his plastic bracelet?'

'We've got a good solid claim for money to be spent on our education project,' said Ellen. 'Leave it with me. I'll edit the film and get an appointment to see Roger at St. Stephens Council. Then I think we should have a team of us go and present our argument.'

'Lucy, will you come with me to speak up for the sea animals?' she asked.

I looked around ... everyone was looking at me.

'You must go,' said Jack. 'You're the one with all the ideas and the one who's pushed for all this. You're the one who understands the turtles.'

I looked at Mum. She was nodding.

'You must finish this off, Lucy.' said Mum. 'Jack's right, you did start all this.'

'Okay,' I said, nodding. 'If it's alright with Mum, then, of course, I'll go with you, Ellen.'

I looked at Dan. 'Will you come too?'

Joel started laughing. 'He'd have to smarten himself up a bit if he wants to go!' he said. 'Seeing someone as scruffy as Dan would frighten everyone. No, Lucy, just let you and Ellen represent us all. You two are quite capable and can speak up for us. We all support you.'

Joel smiled at me and nodded. 'You can do it, Lucy. I know you can. You can convince them.'

He was laughing again, his deep gruff voice resounding around the room. 'I reckon we'll be getting 'em boards up, sooner than an iguana can sneeze!'

I didn't know how long it took an iguana to sneeze, but in the next week, I was amazed at our progress.

Ellen soon edited the film and we went to show Roger the film evidence we'd collected.

A few days later, we were asked back to the St. Stephens' Town Council to put the case again, this time to the Mayor and all the councillors.

As we were leaving the Mayor came over to speak to us.

'You have my promise, Lucy,' he said, 'I will arrange for litter bins on all the beaches in the St. Stephens area in the next few weeks, and I will organise the money for the information panels to be made too.'

'Thank you,' I said. I was almost speechless. He was about to walk away but turned to me again.

'I will keep my promise to you Lucy, believe me,' he said. 'I agree it's so important and I think this is just the beginning. One day I believe the whole of Pontus Island will be plastic-free.'

'Well done, Lucy,' said Ellen, 'that was brilliant. I think you really convinced them when they realised that their holiday trade depended on a clean ocean.'

'Yeah, it was great,' I said to Ellen as we walked down the steps of the Council building. 'I can't wait to tell the others.

CHAPTER THIRTY-FIVE

News Story

My world became crazy as we took every opportunity to speak up for the sea creatures.

Our film was shown on the local television news and someone put the video on social media where it went viral. We heard locals talking about the scheme in Drifters and Sol came back from school one day with the news that there was going to be a school visit to the beach later in the year, once the new information panels had been installed.

At school, I was called into the Head Teacher's office. I thought I was in trouble, but Mrs Marshall was smiling as I entered the room.

'You've been making headlines in the local press, young Lucy,' she said, 'with all your efforts to clean up the beach and the ocean. I understand it was you who took the film we've been seeing on the television about dolphins. The whole school staff and most of the pupils are talking about it. I'm so proud of you for fighting for what you believe in.'

I'd never spoken to Mrs Marshall before and hadn't realised she even knew I existed. I didn't know what to say.

'Do you feel brave enough to stand up in front of the school and talk about what you've managed to achieve?' she asked. 'We have the school prize-giving next week, and I think it would be good if you could tell everyone about how you've learnt to dive and what you think about the animals who live in the ocean.'

To begin with, I didn't think I could do it. Stand up in front of the whole school and speak! No way, that'd be far too scary! But Mrs Marshall encouraged me.

'It would be good for all the pupils to hear your story, and how important it is for us to look after the sea creatures,' she said. 'Our pupils need to understand what you think about the plastic hurting the sea animals. I'm sure you could do it. Everyone would support you.'

Surprisingly, I found myself agreeing to do it.

When I walked back into my classroom Emily whispered. 'Are you in trouble with Mrs Marshall?'

'No,' I said, trying not to laugh. 'Nothing's wrong, but I can't tell you what's happening because it's supposed to be a surprise.' Emily looked shocked, her mouth opened, but no words came out.

She'd obviously not seen our video film on TV and was unaware of all the fuss going on. Still living her life in her own little world. I realised I was now feeling sorry for her. She must be quite a lonely girl as she didn't seem to have any friends and was unaware of the outside world.

'Oh,' said Emily at last. She seemed amazed that I'd had to go to the Headteacher but was not in trouble. She'd probably now assumed that I was not only poor, but also a troublesome child. I didn't bother to straighten out her thoughts. 'You'll understand soon,' I said quietly and settled down to my work.

When I got home, I asked Mum to help me write what I was going to say.

'I think you'll find it easier than you think. Joel has helped you understand the underwater world so much now and your enthusiasm will help you get through it. It would be great if you share it with everyone at school.'

The day of the prize-giving arrived very quickly. It was to be held in the school hall on Friday afternoon. The whole school would be there, and all parents were invited, together with local community leaders. The Mayor would be presenting the prizes.

I would much rather have sat with my friends, but my form teacher insisted I sat in a reserved seat in the front row, close to the stage where I'd go up to speak. As more pupils walked into the hall, the excited murmuring got louder behind me.

It was too scary to turn around ... how many people were coming into the hall? Had my Mum arrived ... was she sitting with all the other parents at the back?

The Headteacher came in with all the special guests and they trooped up the steps and onto the stage. The Mayor was dressed in a blue and gold robe which was so long it touched his shoes. He wore a gold chain of office, which rattled as he walked.

The prize-giving began with certificates being given to pupils to recognise their achievements in geography, history, English, art and science. There were cups and shields awarded to pupils who had excelled at sport and music. Everyone in the hall clapped and cheered as each prize was awarded.

Then Mrs Marshall stood up and addressed the audience.

'St. Stephens's School has been very lucky this year to have a new pupil come to join us. Lucy Morgan has settled into our community really well, and I'm going to ask her to come and talk to us all about what's happened to her in the past few months.'

My knees really were shaking as I went up the steps to the stage. I turned and nearly ran off the stage when I saw how many people were facing me. All the pupils were sitting in rows of chairs in front of me, all quiet and looking up at me expectantly. I glanced to the back but couldn't see Mum in amongst the parents. I hoped she was there somewhere.

CHAPTER THIRTY-SIX

Sharing my Journey

I took a deep breath.

'Coming to live in a different country was a shock,' I said. 'At the beginning everything seemed strange, but so many people have been kind. I've made new friends and now I really feel at home here. The most exciting part has been learning to dive and discovering the sea creatures.'

I explained how being underwater was alien to humans and how diving seemed so scary at first, but then spoke about how I'd come to love the ocean animals. I also told them about the problems with plastic in the oceans and the harm that it was doing. 'Diving has helped me understand the dangers for turtles and other sea life,' I said, 'and I hope our film will help everyone understand the problems caused by rubbish in the ocean.'

I looked across at the Mayor and thanked him for agreeing to help with the rubbish bins on the beach and for organising the information boards.

Then I said out loud what had been in my mind for weeks - that 'Pontus was a pretty good place to live' and the school hall erupted loudly in sound as everyone cheered.

I glanced towards Mrs Marshall, hoping it was time for me to sit down. She came towards me, smiling.

'Thank you, Lucy, for telling us all about your adventures,' she said. 'I'm sure that everyone in the school is as proud of you as I am, for all your hard work to help remove rubbish from the ocean and protect the sea creatures.'

I walked back to my seat as the audience applauded and as I let out a sigh of air ... my cheeks puffed out. Job done. Good. Can I just go back to be a normal pupil again?

I wasn't expecting what happened next.

Mrs Marshall announced that she was going to show our video of the dolphin rescue. The pupils were buzzing with excitement. Some who'd seen it on television were telling their friends how amazing it was and suggesting they should pay attention, but the noise in the school hall turned to silence as the film started ... but it didn't stay quiet for long.

The whole school WATCHED intently as Jack and Sol cut the fishing line away from the dolphin

... they CLAPPED as the net was collected in the RIB

... they CHEERED as the dolphins carried the net to the surface

... and they LAUGHED when Jack called a dolphin 'buddy.'

The Mayor was then invited to speak.

'You might have heard that the St. Stephens' Council is now doing all it can to reduce plastic getting into the oceans, and I hope that in the future the whole of Pontus Island will be free of plastics.' announced the Mayor. The crowded hall came alive with applause once again.

'There are three young people in this school who've made it their mission to stop the use of plastics here, and what they have done has changed the thinking of politicians like me.'

'I congratulate Jack and Solomon on the rescue and Lucy for her camerawork and for ensuring that all three of them returned safely to the surface.'

I didn't dare turn around. I could feel everyone looking at me.

'I would like to announce that we have some extra awards to give out this afternoon,' said the Mayor. 'Awards that we have designed especially for this very special situation.'

'Firstly, a shield that we are calling the Wildlife Award. We are awarding one each to Jack and Solomon for their work in saving the young dolphin from the fishing net.'

Everyone was applauding as Jack and Sol wriggled past pupils' knees and stood on pupil's feet as they exited their row and walked onto the stage to accept their awards. They slapped each other on the back and couldn't stop smiling.

When the applause died down, Jack and Sol were asked to wait at the back of the stage.

The Mayor spoke again.

'And of course, we're not forgetting our heroine in this rescue. I'm happy to announce that St. Stephens' Council has donated a magnificent cup, to be called the Community Award and it is my pleasure to award it to someone who has shown great courage and determination to fight for her beliefs. This award goes to Lucy Morgan.'

I returned to the stage, absolutely astounded at what was happening. I accepted the large silver cup and held it up, like a football captain winning the World Cup!

As I turned to the hall, I could see all the pupils and parents standing. Everybody was clapping and cheering. I could see Emily in the row of my classmates. She was jumping up and down with excitement, and I could hear her shouting, 'Well done, Lucy.' Perhaps she'd learnt something today and maybe now realised that life wasn't all about posh houses and money.

At last, I saw Mum. She was at the back of the hall. I was so pleased to see her there, sharing in everything that was happening. Alongside her were Dan, Joel, Ellen, Jack's Mum and Dad, and Sol's parents too. They were all smiling and applauding. Tears started running down my cheeks.

The Mayor held up his hand and the hall quietened down. Then he spoke loudly so everyone could hear him.

'Lucy,' he said, 'you've been a star in all this. I'm so glad you got me involved with your ideas and delighted that everyone here this afternoon appreciates all your efforts. I'd like to ask you to help the local community by sharing all the benefits of your knowledge of diving and ocean life. You can be our expert witness. I want you to come at any time to the local Council to keep us informed about the environment and any problems you find with ocean creatures. With your help we can try and improve this wonderful Island and its surrounding oceans. I'd like you to help us design a better future for Pontus Island.'

Wow! Join the grown-ups as an expert witness! Help them make future decisions! That's better than giving me a silver cup. I looked to the back of the hall and saw Joel smiling.

'Thank you, Mr Mayor, I'd love to do that.'

He asked me if I wanted to say anything.

I got Jack and Sol to stand beside me and looked at everyone in the hall.

'Thank you, Mr Mayor and Mrs Marshall, for our awards today,' I said. 'We've worked as a team on these ideas, but other people have helped us, and we need to thank them, too. Dan, Joel, and Ellen have been incredibly helpful, and we couldn't have achieved all this without them. We've also had tremendous encouragement from our parents.'

I was looking at my Mum as I spoke. 'My Mum especially has been so supportive, and I couldn't have done any of this without her.'

The audience was clapping again. I saw Mum smiling at Joel and Dan with both hands in the air was holding his thumbs up.

'But it wasn't just us humans, was it,' I said. 'Those dolphins really did a great job at persuading everyone for us, didn't they? I shall never forget that dive. Ever!'

The applause thundered as we went down the steps and I ran to the back of the hall with my special cup and found Mum. We hugged for ages, whilst I wiped away my tears.

'Well done, Lucy. I'm so proud of you,' said Mum. 'Goodness knows what you're going to get up to next!'

'I've no idea, Mum,' I said, 'but judging by what's occurred so far, anything could happen.'

SCIENCE STUFF

Lucy's Dive Equipment

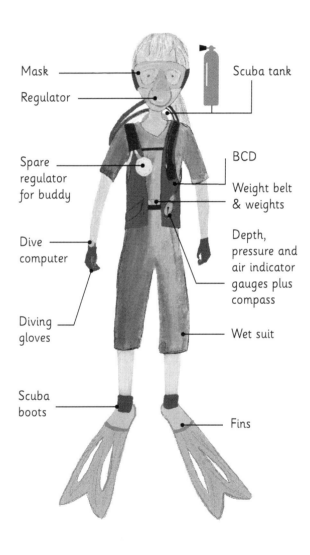

Mask

Regulator

Spare
regulator
for buddy

Dive
computer

Diving
gloves

Scuba
boots

Scuba tank

BCD

Weight belt
& weights

Depth,
pressure and
air indicator
gauges plus
compass

Wet suit

Fins

Chapter 5 - Gecko

Not an underwater creature – but lives in Lucy's new house. A small lizard with special pads on its feet so it can climb up walls and walk across ceilings. It loves to eat the small insects inside houses in warm countries. Harmless and useful.

Chapter 7 - Dolphins

Dolphins are mammals – not fish. They need to come to the surface to breathe air. They are very intelligent and love to play around the bows of a boat.

Chapter 9 - Hawksbill Turtle

Turtles are ocean reptiles – they breathe air from the surface. They can swim at up to thirty miles per hour and stay underwater without breathing for up to five hours. They eat soft coral, crabs and small fish.

Chapter 12 - Moray Eel

Moray eels are fish. There are lots of different species of all colours and sizes. They have elongated bodies and sharp teeth and hunt for small fish who hide in the cracks of the coral reef.

Chapter 15 - Yellow Snappers

Medium size fish with scales and gills. They love to swim together in shoals. This is a protective behaviour which helps them to survive.

Chapter 15 - Cornet Fish

A small elongated fish with a long pipe-like face and tiny fins. It can change colour from grey to yellow, or plain to stripes to help it hide in the coral reef.

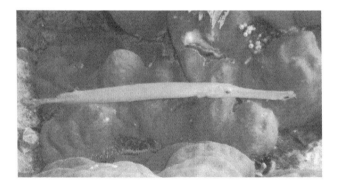

Chapter 15 - Purple Pipe Sponges

Sponges are animals with a tube-like structure – they have cell/tissue layers forming their walls. These tube walls have inner and outer layers of cells which contain sharp, stinging, needle-like projections where microscopic food particles get trapped. The food gets transferred into the middle layer of cells where the food is digested. Sponges are thought to be the oldest multi-celled creatures on Earth.

Chapter 15 - Dome Coral

Dome coral is a species of hard coral, made of calcium carbonate (like human bones). These sturdy corals are made up of thousands of small polyps. Each polyp is a separate animal. When not feeding they look like a pile of stones but when feeding they push out tentacles which catch small plankton as it floats past in the current.

Chapter 15 - Fan Coral

A beautiful coral which takes hundreds of years to form into a shape like this one. It looks like a giant skeleton but is very thin and delicate. All corals are animals, but they don't chase their food like fish do, they wait for the particles of food to float close by and stick to them.

Chapter 15 - Spider Crab

Spider crabs can run fast but they get caught by larger sea creatures like octopus and turtles. They have a shell on the outside of their bodies (exoskeleton), to help protect them. They can chase the small shrimps and fish which they like to eat.

Chapter 16 - Sea Slugs

Most sea slugs have beautiful colours and are nothing like the slimy animals you get in gardens. They have no eyes, but slide slowly over the coral, finding their way using light organs which look like small horns. It can only 'see' light and dark. On top of its body at the back end are its 'lungs' ... a special feathery organ which takes oxygen from the water.

Chapter 16 - Sharks

There are 370 different species of shark ... and only three are dangerous to humans. This is a harmless group of silky sharks happily swimming around together. Sharks are the top predators in the ocean.

Chapter 16 - Manta Ray

Rays and sharks are related as they have a common ancestor, but rays look different as they have formed beautiful wing-like structures which help them move in the water. The manta ray is the largest ray in the ocean. It can measure up to 7 metres across. Its large mouth is at the front of its body.

Chapter 18 - Sergeant Majors

Tiny fish which love to swim in shoals. They usually swim in the top five metres of the ocean. They feed on microscopic algae and plankton which are found in the sunlit areas of the oceans.

Chapter 18 - Soft coral

Soft coral comes in all colours. Soft corals do not have hard calcium carbonate structures like hard coral but are filled with water (a hydro-skeleton) which keeps their shape. Each small dot is an individual coral animal. They are sessile (they don't swim or move around) and they wait for their food to float towards them.

Chapter 22 - Stingray

This is a dangerous animal. This ray species has a sting in its tail. Keep well away!

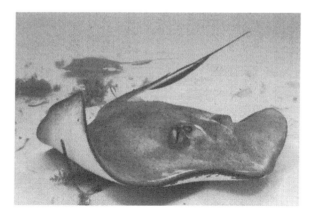

Chapter 22 - Grouper

A large grumpy-looking fish (its mouth goes down at the edges – making it look cross). There are many varieties of grouper – all with different patterns and colours on their bodies.

Chapter 22 - Barracuda

A very big fish, with very big sharp teeth - it has been known to bite diver's fingers. Stay clear of this one.

Chapter 25 - Spadefish

A large graceful fish which swims slowly. It is totally harmless to divers. Often seen in large shoals. It's a spectacular sight when a shoal of these fish swim by.

Chapter 25 - Blue Fusiliers

Always found in shoals, often containing hundreds of fish.

Flashes of blue pass you by – and if you are in the way of the shoal – the fish merely swim over you and around you as they move on through the water.

Chapter 25 - Black-tipped Reef Shark

Quite harmless to divers but awesome to watch. Sharks are really beautiful animals which are perfectly adapted for their environment. Large tails act like engines and sleek bodies move easily through the water. It's always exciting to be swimming alongside reef sharks.

Chapter 25 - Coral (tentacles feeding)

Each hard coral is a separate animal, shaped like a small tube, with tentacles that emerge from the centre, opening and closing to catch the microscopic algae and plankton which they eat. The food is then pushed into the centre of their bodies. Beautiful to watch when feeding.

Chapter 25 - Hawkfish

A medium-sized and very colourful fish which often takes a rest by sitting on hard coral. This one is sitting on staghorn coral where its head is camouflaged. It sits so still a diver rarely sees it but as you get closer the hawkfish darts out from its sitting position and swims away, often making a diver jump because they haven't noticed it.

Chapter 25 - Puffer Fish

There are different species from small to medium-sized. These fish can take water into their bodies and puff themselves up into a ball with the spines on their bodies sticking outwards. This is a defensive mechanism which stops them from being eaten by predatory fish.

Chapter 25 - Wart Slug

Just a beautiful tiny sea slug really – but because it has a bumpy, lumpy look about it – it gets named after a wart (which is a pimply spot on a human face). It is very colourful and is harmless.

Chapter 28 - Butterfly fish

Medium-sized fish – usually swimming around in mating pairs. They mate for life. There are many varieties – this photo shows two masked butterfly fish. Bright yellow with black shading over their eyes which look like a mask.

Chapter 28 - Parrotfish

This fish has a mouthful of very sharp teeth. It eats by scraping algae off the hard coral. It is harmless to divers. There are a number of varieties of this fish all with different colouring. This species is bluey/green – beautiful!

Chapter 28 - Jellyfish

Have no bones or brains! They have an undulating movement of their tentacles which keep them up towards the surface. They have algae inside them which need to make food from the sun (photosynthesis – like plants do on land). Jellyfish are the favourite food of turtles.

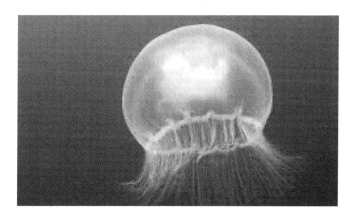

Chapter 32 - Crab

Famous for being able to walk sideways, crabs have an exoskeleton (bony shell on the outside of their bodies). They have sticky-out eyes and sharp claws. Very fast at running if they climb out of the ocean and run across the rocks. This crab is from the Galapagos Islands – and is incredibly colourful.

Chapter 32 - Dolphins
Intelligent animals who swim together in family groups called pods. They love to play in the water with divers and are very streamlined which allows them to swim fast. They can travel up to 500 miles a day in oceans all around the world.

Chapter 5 - Zebbie

He may not be a real 'animal' but he's very special to Lucy.

These photographs have been taken at different places around the world.

All photos © copyright to the author

THE LUCY MORGAN ADVENTURE SERIES
(for ages 8-12 years)

Book 1. Eye of the Turtle
Book 2. The Secret of the Shallows

The Secret of the Shallows is due to be published in September 2020

Reviews for 'The Secrets of the Shallows'

From Dylan (age 10)

'This is an excellent book that lots of children would love to read, with a moral to it. I think it's fantastic to write a fictional book based on real facts, as it really inspires people to save the sea creatures, just like Lucy, Jack and Solomon are doing. The first book 'Eye of the Turtle' took me two weeks to read, but this new one only took just over a week. I think I enjoyed Book 2 even more than Book 1 and I didn't think that was possible. These two books are some of the best I've read in a long time, and definitely the quickest book I've ever read! I thoroughly enjoyed this book and I hope there will be more in the series. My favourite part about this book is that there are always cliff-hangers. I JUST CAN'T STOP READING IT!!'

From Lily, (age 12)

"A thrilling read with another great story line this is a spectacular sequel to the extraordinary 'Eye of the Turtle'. With the same loveable characters, this time facing a new set of challenges, what more could you ask for in a book? Without doubt, I strongly rate this a 10/10"

To find **FREE Activity Sheets**
... go to the Kid's pages on the author's website at
www.barnettauthor.co.uk

A *Free Gift* from the author:

If you'd like to see any creature from the photo glossary in
FULL COLOUR
then send an email to gloria@barnettauthor.co.uk
(telling me which sea creature you'd like to have)
– and I will send a download of the photo to your email address.
You will be able to use the glossary picture as screensaver or print it off to put into your journal or to have on your wall at home or in school.

All photos are © copyright to the author – so you won't be allowed to print them off and sell them to your friends - or use them in your own incredible published book in the future!

Your email address will be used for sending you the photo plus information about new books in this series in the future.

Your email details will be looked after and never shared with anyone else.

REVIEWS

If you purchased your book through AMAZON, then you can also write a review on their website – just go back to the AMAZON page where you purchased this book and add your review.
Your review gets published on the Amazon book page and could be read by millions of people around the world.

CONTACT THE AUTHOR

email
gloria@barnettauthor.co.uk

ACKNOWLEDGEMENTS

The author's thanks go to:

My family: Chris, my husband and special dive buddy, together with Matthew, Hannah and Rebecca's families, the Thomas's, the James's and the Barnett's who understood the need to share my love of oceans and supported me every step of the way.

Andrew Lamb who pushed, shoved and kicked me into writing fiction and then gave me enormous encouragement and insight as I honed my skills.

Katrin Lamb for her incredible illustrations

Silva, Jane and Christine for reading early versions and not laughing too much when my stories seemed more like absurd manuals for learning to dive.

David Sanger for all his encouragement in the early stages.

Celia Rumley at Amber designs for sharing her amazing creativity

Rochelle for my website and Pauline for the proofreading

The adults and children who have given their opinions as reviewers.

The Rotary friends who invited me to talk at conferences and clubs, allowing me to share my passion for the oceans.

Charity organisers and everyone who lets me talk to their audiences.

The many cruise passengers who became friends and having listened to my lectures, then insisted that I write children's fiction.

... and last but not least Ryby and Tracy Stonehouse who patiently taught me how to dive and introduced me to the wonderful underwater world.

Thank you - everyone.

ABOUT THE AUTHOR

For over 30 years Gloria has been exploring our planet's oceans and has dived in a variety of areas around the world. She is a master scuba diver, keen sailor and underwater videographer as well as an educational advisor, science presenter and author.

Gloria visits schools in her guise as the 'WeirdFish Lady' presenting 'Underwater Adventure Days' inspiring and encouraging learning about
the natural world.

Contact Gloria at
gloria@barnettauthor.co.uk

Remember:
- there is only one planet Earth
- it is our home
- help to look after it!

Teacher's Resource for ages 8 - 12

For Primary Schools, Secondary KS3, Science Clubs, Home Learning and anywhere elsewhere children want to learn.

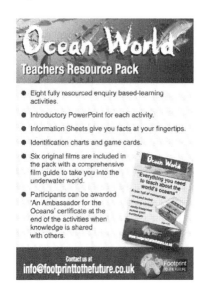

Available now
at www.footprinttothefuture.co.uk

Footprint to the Future is a social enterprise
producing teaching resources and books
to help everyone understand
Planet Earth.
Gloria is the lead science writer for this enterprise.

Printed in Poland
by Amazon Fulfillment
Poland Sp. z o.o., Wrocław

58811272R00106